Simon Says

Simon Says

Brenda C. Poulos

Printed in the United States of America
Published by Author Academy Elite
P.O. Box 43, Powell, OH 43035

www.AuthorAcademyElite.com

ISBN: 978-1-64085-198-6
ISBN: 978-1-64085-199-3

Library of Congress Control Number: 2018938210

Author Academy Elite, Powell, OH

To Promise, Skylare, Liberty, Sylas, Owen,
Madison, and Liliana.

Grandchildren are among God's greatest blessings.
Each of you are beautiful, unique,
and very special.

Love,
Grandma

Acknowledgements

My sincere thanks to my Beta Readers and my critique group members for their encouragement, suggestions, and insight. Their comments were invaluable in making *Simon Says* heartfelt and genuine.

Crystal Acosta
Sue DeMets
Chalona Fensler
Nancy Johnson
Linda Phar

"Save me, O God, for the floodwaters are up to my neck. Deeper and deeper I sink into the mire; I cannot find a foothold to stand on. I am in deep water, and the floods overwhelm me."

Psalm 69: 1-2

Prologue

Celia turned her attention from the newborn son sleeping peacefully in her arms to meet her husband's dark eyes. "I'm sorry…so, so sorry, Lincoln."

His face reddened as he replied through clenched teeth. "I begged you. I pleaded with you. We both knew this might happen."

Celia reached out to touch her husband's hand. "I haven't had a drink in over a month. Doesn't that count for something?"

Lincoln jerked away. "I'm glad you've quit—at least for the time being—but the change is a little too late, don't you think?" He brought his shirtsleeve up to his eyes and wiped them, dampening the worn denim cuff. "Too late for our boy, Celia. If he lives, he'll struggle to walk, talk, and learn like normal kids. And all because of your obsession with booze."

"It'll turn out all right. You'll see."

"Look at him, Celia. Are you blind, girl? All the signs Doc talked about are there—short nose, small eyes, thin upper lip. The surgery for the cleft palate, alone, will leave us with not a cent to our name." He hung his head, shoulders heaving, as he cried.

"I—I don't know what to say." She looked down at the baby, stroking his soft reddish-gold hair with her thumb. She unfolded his fingers and inspected the tiny nails. Tears fell as she brushed his smooth belly with the back of her hand and gently kissed the bottoms of his feet.

Lincoln shook his head, dropped an empty plastic cup in the trash and headed for the door. "I'll be gone by the time you're discharged. I'll ask a neighbor to make sure you get home okay."

"You're leaving me…us?" Her wet cheeks glistened in the light from the bedside lamp. "Don't you even want to hold him? He's your son!" Her breath caught as he hesitated at the door.

"Don't name him after me."

Part One

I pray to you, Lord,
in the time of your favor;
in your great love, O God,
answer me with your sure salvation.

Rescue me from the mire,
do not let me sink;
deliver me from those who hate me,
from the deep waters.

Do not let the floodwaters engulf me
or the depths swallow me up
or the pit close its mouth over me.

Answer me, Lord, out of the goodness of your love;
in your great mercy turn to me.

Psalm 69: 13-16

Chapter One

The door clicked shut, followed by the familiar screech of the screen door.

Marcus pulled the sheer olive-green curtain back, watching as Mama slipped behind the wheel of the 1962 Impala. He waved in response to the grin she cast over her shoulder.

She backed the car into the street, wiggled her fingers at him and sped away.

Mama worked the night shift—even on Fridays.

Marcus let the curtain fall back in place and turned off the hallway light. He crossed the floor to the kitchen, removing a chair from its place at the table. He dragged it toward his bedroom, its legs following the deep grooves that his nightly ritual had worn into the wood over the years. He placed it in front of the narrow window, sat down and crossed his forearms on the sill.

He reached for Baxter, his miniature gray Schnauzer, and hauled him onto his lap. Lowering his chin to rest on top of his hands, he scanned the street to the left and then the right. The boys would be coming out soon. They always played ball after supper. First, Rex and his brother, Bill, would show up. Then, Abel, followed by Archie, and finally Simon. They'd meet at the bend in the street, just as Forrest turned into Cornell, directly in front of his house.

This had always been a good vantage point for Marcus, enabling him to see in both directions...and close enough, too, to detect the smug expressions on the boys' faces when they got a good hit, or the defeat in their eyes when a strike was called. But no matter how well the other boys played, the hour of baseball after supper each weekday night would end the same way. Simon would declare himself the victor and that was that.

Marcus knew that Simon really wasn't the winner *every* time. But instead of protesting, the other boys would just shrug their shoulders and walk back home.

Maybe they were afraid of Simon. Marcus knew *he* sure was.

He and Mama had lived in Tempe, Arizona for ten years now. Mama had been so proud when she had saved enough for the down payment, signed the papers, and dropped the shiny new key into his hand. "We're moving into our own place, Marcus. You'll have your own bedroom and, I hope, some children your own age to play with."

He hadn't needed a room of his own. He'd been happy enough, having slept on Granny's fold-out sofa with Mama for the first seven years of his life. *What had been the big deal about them having their own home?* He liked the way things were before—playing checkers with Gramps, romping in the back yard with their miniature Schnauzer, Baxter, and eating Granny's home cooking.

Now, at seventeen, Marcus could barely remember what his grandparents had looked like. Not long after he and Mama moved, Gramps had died from a bad case of pneumonia. Granny died later that spring. Uncle Dwayne had inherited their house, Mama the Impala, and Baxter had been left to Marcus.

He turned his attention back outside as first one boy, then another, met under the street light. Rex and Abel paired up, tossing the ball back and forth into each other's gloved hands. Bill and Archie did the same. *Where was Simon?*

Marcus looked at the digital clock on his nightstand. He sighed. Seven-fifteen. Nothing exciting was going to happen tonight. Not without Simon. Opening his arms wide, he stretched and headed for the refrigerator to retrieve a leftover piece of Mama's apple pie.

It was then that a shiny red car drove past, drawing his attention back toward the window. As it pulled into the driveway next door, the boys cast aside their gloves and crowded around. Simon emerged, all smiles, amid cheers from his buddies. The next few minutes were spent with Simon showing the vehicle off. Then, after a nod from his father, all of the boys packed into the car and it took off down the road.

What about the game?

"Things are changing, Marcus. The guys are dating now. That will take up more and more of their evenings. I suppose it's only natural."

Marcus heard the words his mother said the following morning, but he didn't understand why things had to change just because everyone was getting older.

He gripped his mother's arm. "But, Mama, baseball is better than girls."

She patted his hand with her soapy one. "They'll still play now and then. You'll see."

"But, Mama—"

"How about you dry the lunch dishes for me, huh?" Mama held up a soapy plate, dunked it into the rinse water, and thrust it toward Marcus.

As he dried the dish and placed it in the cupboard, he heard the faint but familiar calliope music from the ice cream truck. Turning toward his mother, he smiled; then raised his eyebrows. "Can I?"

Mama wiped her hands on her apron. "We have ice cream in the freezer. I'm afraid you've gotten too old for—"

"Please, Mama." Marcus had already taken the money jar from its place on the counter and was holding it out toward her.

She bit her lip. "All right." She opened the jar, dropping her tip money onto the palm of his hand.

He scurried down the steps and ran to the end of the street, Mama following along behind, as had been her custom over the years. "Be careful not to run the smaller children over," she called.

He loved getting ice cream from Mr. Jerry, the ice cream man, although it had not always been a pleasant experience for him. Simon had begun taunting Marcus just a few days after they moved into the neighborhood, on Marcus's very first visit to the truck.

He had run ahead of Mama, just as he had today, smiling and holding up the shiny quarter for all the world to see. "Thank you, Mama." His voice trailed off as he reached the growing line of neighborhood children in front of the brightly painted vehicle.

Just as Mr. Jerry placed the strawberry cone in his hand, someone pushed from behind. Marcus fell against the red and white truck, the cone crumbling in his fingers and ice cream plopping onto the sidewalk. He stood in front of the small sliding window, staring at the mess, saliva drooling down his chin.

Mama walked forward, pulled a handkerchief from her waistband and wiped the pink concoction off his hand. Dropping to her knees, she sopped up the melting treat from the sidewalk.

As snickers drifted from the rear of the line, Mama gritted her teeth, then grabbed Marcus's hand, leading him past Simon The Bully (as he came to be known), across the lawn and up the porch steps of their small bungalow.

Marcus leaned his back against the door, and hung his head, hot tears trickling down his cheeks. When he heard the familiar clink against the mouth of the special treat jar, he swiped at his eyes. He blinked as Mama's fingers retrieved the last quarter. She held his hand and half-dragged him down the street, falling in at the end of the line. "Just look straight ahead, son," she whispered.

"Hey, Lickenbooger, what happened to your cone?" Simon sneered.

"I—I"

Mama jerked his hand. "Marcus!"

Marcus put his fingers to his lips, turning the key to an imaginary lock.

Mama's eyes beaded on Simon's mischievous grin. "I don't want to have to report your poor behavior to your mama."

Simon glared at her; then turned at last to face forward. He hissed over his shoulder. "What a little baby you are. Can't take a joke? Always need your mama to rescue you from bad boys like me?"

Marcus looked forward to the start of the second semester. New classes always held the hope of making a new friend. Both he and Mama had included that request in their prayers every morning at breakfast for as long as he could remember.

The day had gotten off to a bad start. His third period special P.E. class had been paired with the regular class for football. Although Marcus was awkward—both physically and socially—he was of average intelligence and not technically a special kid. He understood why he'd always been lumped in with them, though. It was because of his physical abnormalities—upturned nose, somewhat small head and eyes.

He'd recently compared his class photo with earlier ones in Mama's picture album. Was it his imagination, or was he almost handsome? His face had filled out a bit and the scar from his cleft lip was no longer discolored, leaving an almost translucent—albeit jagged and slightly raised—scar. But long ago he'd been labeled in the "system" and Mama said there was nothing that could be done to change it.

The coach, Ryan Nichols, had been his P.E. teacher last year, too. He never laughed at or belittled any of the guys, regular or special. Whether they were uncoordinated or star athletes, he treated them all the same.

Marcus turned in the direction of laughter down the hall. He couldn't face Simon and the others in the small locker room. He tossed his clothes inside number thirty-eight and snapped the padlock shut. He hung the lanyard with the key over his neck, letting it drop inside his shirt, and headed for the door.

Once on the field, he nodded at Robbie. So far, he was the only other special kid he'd seen out there. He hoped they'd end up on the same team. It would be great to have someone to talk to.

It had been his fourth year of school before he'd spoken a word to anyone, being self-conscious about his difficulty pronouncing r's and l's. However, his speech had slowly improved and now he only had trouble when he was nervous or upset. *I don't get it. The special students understand me just fine. Why do the "regular" ones still tease me?*

Coach Nichols jogged onto the field, blowing his whistle and motioning for everyone to join him at third base. "All right, men, everyone move in close. I'll be assessing your skill levels this week. We'll start with a short game. Simon and Freddie, you'll be captains." He took a quarter from his pocket and threw it high into the air. When he caught it, he flipped it onto the back of his hand and covered it with his other one. "Call it, Freddie."

"Heads."

The boys crowded around the coach as he uncovered the coin. "Tails. Simon, you choose first."

Everyone yelled for Simon to choose him. He took his time, and so did Freddie, emphasizing the fact that they had been singled out as leaders, puffing out their chests as they strutted in front of the class.

After a lengthy back and forth, the teams were formed, with only Robbie and Marcus remaining on the bench.

"Come on, boys, choose your last man," the coach ordered.

Simon scowled. "I'm done."

Coach Nichols squinted his eyes. "Choose, now, or I'll choose for you."

Marcus lowered his head, looking down at the scuffed rubber toes of his tennis shoes, broken shoestrings barely reaching far enough to knot together. They had been his school shoes last year. Now, they'd become his P.E. shoes. His heart pounded as he waited.

"Lickenbooger."

His head snapped up. Had that been Simon's voice, choosing *him?* His eyes met Simon's. With a big grin on his face, he hustled over to his team, amid their laughter. He didn't care what Simon had called him. He had been picked. "Gee, thanks, Simon."

Simon stepped forward. He lowered his voice, talking out of the side of his mouth as he often did. "Don't think you're here by choice. Robbie's leg is in a cast. I'd be an idiot to choose him."

Chapter Two

To Marcus's surprise, the week went by quickly. On Friday afternoon, he rummaged through the items at the sidewalk sale in front of Hamilton's Hardware. A screwdriver, a couple of tape measures. Same stuff as last week.

He pushed his bike past two older men playing checkers at a table outside a gift store on his way to pick up a few things at the market for Mama. He stopped dead in his tracks outside the Goodwill Store where a Spider-Man costume was displayed front and center.

His heart began to pound as he took in every detail—the web on the front…the matching mask. Ten dollars. His old costume no longer fit him… He shoved his hand into the pocket of his jeans, pulling out the grocery list and the ten-dollar bill clipped to it. He drew in a sharp breath.

Before he knew it, he'd pushed open the door and was running his fingertips over the silken fabric.

Marcus lay back against the softness of the sofa pillow, stretching as the Spider-Man movie neared his favorite part. He watched the same movie every Friday night, accompanied by Baxter, and a large bowl of popcorn. However, tonight his mother had put the Halloween candy in the bowl—with strict instructions not to eat any of it until after he turned off the porch light at nine o'clock.

He checked the contents of the bowl, hoping there would be enough candy to last the rest of the evening. A lot of kids had been by already. They had been a constant interruption to his movie, but he enjoyed seeing their Halloween costumes.

When the doorbell rang again, he grabbed the bowl of candy and headed for the door. He flung it open, Baxter following to growl at a trio of Ninja Turtles standing on the porch steps.

"Trick or treat!" All three bent over, laughing and pointing. "Who are *you* supposed to be?" The tallest ninja walked forward, reaching into the bowl to help himself to the last of the Tootsie Rolls.

Marcus frowned, looking down at his costume. "Spider-Man, of course."

"You're not Spider-Man." The ninjas skittered off the steps and headed down the driveway.

"I am so." Marcus called after them, heat rising under his mask.

One ninja paused at the end of the driveway. "You're a fake."

His rapid heartbeat left Marcus feeling lightheaded. His slammed the door shut and turned out the light. Heading to the kitchen, he ripped off his Spider-Man mask and flipped on the switch to the air popper.

He'd been Peter Parker, Mary Jane's hero, ever since he was four. Mama had stayed up late nights for almost a week sewing his costume on the old treadle sewing machine in Granny's basement. She finished the night before Halloween.

"I'm Spider-Man, the greatest superhero of all." He turned around several times, admiring himself in his grandmother's ornate full-length mirror. "I'm going to save Mary Jane from the evil—"

"I have something else for you, too," his grandfather interrupted. "Close your eyes and hold out your arm."

Marcus couldn't help peeking as Gramps strapped a Spider-Man watch around his wrist. "Wow! This is the best day of my life."

Marcus sat on the steps outside the front door, his knees drawn up to his chest and his head resting in his hands. The two policemen that had been trying to make sense of his story—the reason he had called for them thirty minutes earlier—looked up when Mama screeched the Impala to a halt in the driveway.

She left the engine running as she rushed up the cement incline toward Marcus. "What's going on? I got a call at work from the police department." Mama's blotchy face left no doubt that she'd been crying.

Marcus pointed toward the side of the house, raw eggs still oozing down the stucco.

"This is why you called the police? Marcus, this was *not* an emergency."

Marcus ran his fingers through his hair. "The trick-or-treaters did this. They said I wasn't Spider-Man. They came back later and—"

Mama thrust her palm forward. "Enough. I don't want to hear it." She turned to the officers, her shoulders stooped and her face red.

"It's all right, Ma'am. We've been here before. We know he's getting older, but maybe he still shouldn't be left alone at night." The policemen walked toward their patrol car, shaking their heads.

"Thank you, officers." Mama turned her attention to Marcus. "Get in the house. Go to bed. No candy. We'll talk about this in the morning. I'm heading back to the diner. You'd better hope this doesn't get me fired." Mama's exit was as abrupt as her entrance.

Marcus walked slowly up the steps. If Mama lost her job, it would be his fault. He sighed as he reached for the doorknob.

"Hey, Marcus, do you have any more candy?" A cute ballerina in a sparkling pink tutu, twirled up the driveway.

"Hi, Sheila." He took the hand his neighbor offered and laughed as she curtsied. "I like your crown."

"Thanks. I like your costume, too. Spider-Man is my favorite."

"Mine, too." He hung his head. "I'm sorry, but I don't have any more candy."

"Mrs. Perkins was out of candy, too. She gave me a dime instead." Her eyes grew round as she looked up at him. "See?" She held up the shiny coin.

Marcus bit his lip. "Just a minute." He ran into the house, picked up the treat jar and gave it a shake. It was empty. He'd spent the last of the money on yesterday's ice cream. Frowning, his hand brushed against one of Mama's envelopes as he replaced the lid. He snatched the one labeled "utilities" and let the contents fall into his hand.

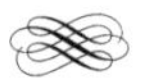

Sweat rolled down Marcus's face as he made another pass with the lawnmower. Grass sure did grow fast... especially in the fall, right after what was known in Arizona as the monsoon season. He spent every Saturday morning in the front yard, trimming, mowing, and watering. Then, there was the sweeping up and hauling off the trimmings. By two o'clock in the afternoon, he was beat.

His head turned at the sound of Simon's new car pulling up to the curb. *I wonder if I'll ever get a license... drive a car...*

Simon motioned Marcus over. "Hey, I hear you were pretty generous to a certain little trick-or-treater last night."

"What do you mean?"

"I heard you gave that little Wallace girl down the street a twenty-dollar bill. Is that true?" Simon slapped the palms of his hands against the steering in time with the new Beatles hit blasting on the car radio.

"Yeah. So?" Marcus focused his eyes on the bright red paint of the car, hesitant to let his them meet Simon's.

"Well, now that I know you've got plenty of money, I expect payment on your fines." Simon's eyebrows raised making his words seem like a question, but Marcus had heard that tone of voice before…it sounded more like a demand.

"I don't have any money. I took it from Mama's bill envelope."

"No problem. You can just continue to steal from Mama and pay me back for years of failing to follow my orders."

A door slammed as Simon's father came outside to get his newspaper. Simon pulled away from the curb and into his own driveway. "Don't forget what we talked about, Marcus," he yelled through the open window. "I'm going to be needing date money real soon."

Marcus tossed and turned as he tried to get to sleep later that evening. He had gone to bed with Simon's threats on his mind. He couldn't steal from Mama again. It was wrong. He knew that. He dreaded seeing her tears when she found out.

But, he couldn't bear to disappoint Sheila. After all, that little girl seemed to truly like him—maybe the only one on his street that actually did—and just seeing her smile at him on the way to the bus stop each morning was worth any punishment Mama might give him. And there was no doubt she would once she noticed the electric payment was missing.

He sat up, rubbed his eyes, and walked toward the window. Looking toward the Wilsons' driveway, he stared at Simon's car. It reminded him of the first time Simon and the other boys had allowed him to play the game of Simon Says with them.

Being invited had never seemed to be in the realm of possibility, so when the boys rang the doorbell and told him that he had earned the right to be a member of their group, his head had spun. All of Mama's teachings—warnings, really—went out the window. He couldn't run down the steps fast enough.

At first, Simon's orders were easy to follow. "Pat your stomach. Touch the tip of your nose. Stick out your tongue." But then he got that cold look in his eyes that Marcus had come to know over the years. Mischievous? No. Devilish. Definitely. It had scared Marcus, then. Truth was, it still made his skin crawl.

"Spit on the sidewalk." Simon's lip curled upward at the corner.

Marcus took a step backward. "I'm not supposed to—"

"Let me explain something to you, shrimp. When Simon says to do something, it's an order you don't refuse. Either do it or face the consequences."

Marcus gulped. He didn't know why he looked back at the living room window. Mama was at work. He inched his foot forward, heart pounding, as he walked toward the place on the sidewalk where Simon was pointing. He watched with disgust as Rex, Archie, Abel, and Bill cleared their throats and then dropped huge wads of spit onto the concrete.

"See how easy that is? Your turn." Simon's nostrils flared, his eyes narrowing as he waited.

Marcus sucked hard, but his mouth was dry. He deposited the small amount of saliva he could muster on top of their slimy mound.

When Simon nodded, accepting his offering, Marcus let out a long sign of relief.

"Now, pick up a rock and throw it at that cat over there." Simon pointed over his shoulder to a scrawny tabby lying on top of the Oldsmobile parked in Simon's driveway.

"I don't want to, Simon." Marcus backed up, tripping over the low wire barrier between his yard and Simon's.

"Remember about the consequences, you pathetic little—"

Marcus pulled himself to his knees, reached out for a small rock, and rose to his feet. "Okay, okay." His cheeks burned, a single tear escaping from underneath his thick lashes. He brushed it away with the back of his hand.

"Bigger. Get that one over there." Simon pointed to a black, fist-sized rock lying near the fire hydrant.

His hand shook as Marcus let the pebble fall to the ground.

Simon grabbed the back of his neck and squeezed. "Throw it, you hear me? No more stalling."

Marcus closed his eyes. *Sorry, Mama.* Before he knew it, he'd picked up the rock and hurled it in the direction of the cat that took off at the sound of breaking glass. He'd missed it, but the rock had shattered Mr. Wilson's car window.

The other boys scattered, but Simon stayed around to watch as his father raced outside, took hold of Marcus's ear and twisted. "Just wait 'til your mother gets home, mister. If she doesn't give you a beating, you can bet I will."

Chapter Three

Celia's hands shook as she clutched the utility envelope. She brought her forehead down to rest on the kitchen table. Her son had stolen from her twice. He had called the police unnecessarily on Halloween night. What was getting into him? He'd always been such a good boy—helpful, truthful, and generous to a fault. Hearing him shuffle down the hall, she raised her head and brushed the crumbs off her nose.

"Oops!" Marcus started to back out of the room as he saw her.

"Sit." Celia pointed to the chair next to hers.

Marcus walked around the chair, instead, and took a seat across from her. His eyes were red and swollen.

Celia took a deep breath. She loved him more than anything—anyone—and had felt that way from the first moment she held him. He might not look beautiful to anyone else, but to her he was a miracle and a dream come true.

The years that followed his birth had been a struggle, financially, and emotionally. Living with her parents hadn't been easy, since Daddy continually spoke his mind, sharing his opinions about what "should have been done" each time she asked to borrow money or was too exhausted to help with the housecleaning.

"Daddy, he's my responsibility. I'll take care of him. It's my fault he was born this way. Maybe someday God will forgive me…maybe Lincoln will, too."

"It looks to me like your ma and me are the ones that's payin' the biggest price, here." He opened the desk drawer and took out the worn leather ledger. He'd used it previously to list her mother's income from taking in laundry and ironing, but now her father used it to record Celia's debts—ones he expected to be paid down to the last penny.

He unfolded his spectacles, placing them on his nose and hooking them over his smallish ears. Then he switched on the desk lamp and flipped past more than half of the pages until he found the last entry. "Fourteen hundred dollars, to be exact, Missy."

She gulped. Here it was again—the weekly accounting…the humbling…the tears. "Most of that was for his cleft lip surgery, glasses, and speech therapy. With paying for our room and board, I'm not left with anything—" She twisted her hands in her lap. She appreciated all that her parents had done for them, but the constant reminder of her shortcomings was often more than she could bear.

"Your drinking and lying to your husband got you into this mess. You've got to somehow dig yourself out of it." He thrust out his hand, wiggling his fingers. "Let's have it."

She laid five ten-dollar bills onto his calloused palm. The fifteen dollars she had left had to stretch two weeks.

Celia and her son lived paycheck to paycheck. All she had to show for it was the love in her boy's eyes.

But it was enough.

It had always been.

"Mama—"

"Get a tissue, Marcus. Clean your nose and face before you talk, please."

Marcus did as he was told, depositing the soggy Kleenex into the garbage can. He slunk back into his chair. "Mama, I didn't mean to steal the grocery money. One minute I saw the costume and the next minute I was home putting it on. I had to be Spider-Man, Mama, I just had to."

"I know, son. I understand. But do you realize that now we have no groceries? What are we going to eat the rest of the week, Marcus?"

His eyes brightened. "Soup."

"We'll have to have dry cereal for breakfast and soup for dinner for an entire week. There won't even be milk for macaroni and cheese."

"I'm sorry, Mama. I won't ever do it again." He wiped his runny nose with the sleeve of his shirt.

"But you've already done it again. Or have you forgotten about the utility envelope?" She pushed it across the table. "What happened to the money that was in here?"

"I—I—gave it to Sheila." His eyes remained focused on the crumpled paper.

She took a sip of water, then moistened her lips before she spoke. "What on earth for?"

"The ninjas took the last of the candy."

Celia pushed her chair back and stood up, running her fingers through her hair. If she cancelled her haircut appointment, she could use the money to make the utility payment. Or maybe she could swallow her pride and talk with Sheila's father. "I'm sick with disappointment, Marcus. You're grounded for one month. No bike riding. No ice cream from the truck. And the costume is going up on your closet shelf. You're not to touch it. Understand?"

Marcus kicked a pebble down the sidewalk as he headed home. He missed riding his bike to and from school. It took a lot longer to walk the two miles. It probably didn't matter much, anyhow. There was no reason to rush since he'd been grounded from television when Mama found him sneaking his costume down, yesterday, "just to have a look." It was sure to be a long evening since Mama worked four hours longer on Wednesdays.

As the toe of his tennis shoe met the rock again, he noticed something shiny at the edge of the pavement. He reached down, scratching in between the gravel in a flowerbed and the sidewalk. When his fingers pulled out a quarter, he couldn't believe his luck. If he hurried…

"Hey, whatcha got there, Lickenbooger?" Simon reached over his shoulder and snatched the coin from his hand before Marcus even had a chance to turn around. "This is a pleasant surprise. I didn't expect to get any money out of you quite so soon."

"That's mine, Simon. Give it back." Marcus's face turned red, veins bulging on the side of his neck.

"I don't think so. I've got a date with Sally Schwartz Friday night. She's really cute and I plan to impress her with the very best. Every penny—I mean quarter—will help." Simon raised one eyebrow as he returned to the three jocks waiting for him in the backseat of his nearby convertible. "Thanks, buddy."

Buddy? He's no friend of mine. He picked up the rock he'd been kicking and hurled it at a metal garbage container on the curb. It hit directly in the middle of its side with a loud clank. He laughed in spite of himself. If only he could pitch a baseball like that.

All of a sudden, he was knocked from behind. He sprawled onto the sidewalk, the contents of his backpack spilling into the gutter. He pulled himself up in time to see a kid jump into the front seat of Simon's car.

Simon, Patrick, and their friends talked excitedly, tossing something back and forth to each other—a lively game of Hot Potato. A minute later, Simon jumped out of the car and headed back in Marcus's direction. "Hey, Marcus...Pal, I've got a favor to ask of you."

Marcus wrinkled his nose. *Pal?* "A favor?"

"Yeah. I'll give you back your quarter if you'll do a small thing for me in return. What do you say?"

"I—I—guess so. What is it?" Marcus's heartbeat accelerated. He'd get the quarter back. He'd surprise Mama with a pint of milk.

"All you've got to do is hide this bag in your room for a few days and give it back to Colin when he asks for it. It's a secret—a big surprise for his girlfriend—so no telling. Okay?" Simon thrust a brown paper bag into Marcus's backpack, covering it with the spilled contents from the roadway. Smiling, he placed the backpack onto Marcus's shoulders. "See you around, buddy. Head for home, now, and remember this is our secret." He slapped the quarter into his hand.

There it was, '*buddy*', again. He looked behind him as Simon turned the key in the ignition and peeled out in the opposite direction.

Celia dragged herself through the door a few minutes before midnight. The long hours today and lack of sleep the night before had worn her out. She could think of nothing else than getting into bed. She walked into the kitchen and turned on the light over the range hood so as not to wake Marcus. When she opened the refrigerator and reached for the jug of water, she noticed a pint of milk sitting on top of a folded piece of paper.

She wiggled the paper out from underneath, unfolded it, and read the neatly-printed note:

Mama, this is for your cereal in the morning.
Marcus
XOXOXOXOXOX

Tears trickled down her cheeks. This was the kind of thing Lincoln would have done. How could Marcus be so much like his father when he'd never even lived with him? It was little things like this that reminded her of why she'd fallen in love with Lincoln, why she still cared and why she continued to pray that someday he'd return.

She clicked off the light and made her way down the hallway guided by the moonlight filtering through the thin curtains. When she passed her son's room, she paused, watching his chest rise and fall with each rhythmic breath.

A child in a teenager's body.

The loose glass in the front door rattled in response to a series of loud knocks early Saturday morning. Marcus jumped out of bed and ran the short distance to the living room. He pulled the drape back, peering out the side window. *Simon. What's he doing here?* He grasped the handle, opened the door, and put a finger to his lips. "Shhhh. Mama's still sleeping—I hope."

Simon shifted from one foot to the other and leaned in close. "How's that package I gave you? Hidden, like we discussed?"

"Yeah." Marcus gasped as his eyes met Simon's. Black eye…cut and swollen lip. "What happened? Were you in a fight?"

"Mind your own business, four eyes." Simon tilted his head toward his house and pulled his shirt collar up around his neck. "If you're going to be a member of our group, you've got to learn to keep your trap shut."

Marcus's eyes widened. "I—I'm in your group?"

"Well, it isn't official yet. You still have to get initiated. Do things to prove yourself worthy, you know."

"Like what?"

Simon's eyes darted toward his house, then back to Marcus. "Meet me outside when you see my folks leave. They're going off somewhere this morning with Dad's friends from work. We can get your initiation done while they're gone."

Marcus rolled his eyes. "I'm grounded. Remember?"

Simon grabbed Marcus's shirt collar with a tight fist and pulled him onto the porch. "Listen, squirt, I'm doing you a favor. You think the other guys want you in the club? Of course not. But I've been sticking up for you and now you need to show them you've got what it takes to stand up to your mama."

Simon flinched when his father opened the screen door and yelled in his "Sergeant's" voice. "Get in the house, Simon. I want a word with you."

"Yes, sir." Sweat beaded on Simon's forehead. He turned to go, glaring back at Marcus. "Keep watch. You have your orders—that is, if you want to be a member."

"I do. But—"

Marcus watched Simon jump the hedge and run across the lawn to his house. Once there, a hand yanked him inside. Before he closed the door, he heard Simon's father yelling something about Saturday chores. Maybe Marcus wouldn't have to face the initiation today, after all...

Marcus looked up from his bowl of Cheerios when Mama entered the kitchen. "Morning, Mama."

She kissed the top of Marcus's head. "Thank you for the milk, son." Grabbing the carton from the top shelf of the refrigerator, she poured the milk onto the cereal Marcus had already scooped into her bowl. "Where did you get the money for it?"

"I found it on the sidewalk on the way home from school."

"Well, it was very thoughtful of you to buy the milk. I appreciate it, Marcus." She reached her hand over to pat his arm. "Frannie's relatives are visiting from Omaha. I'm going to work the breakfast shift at the diner so she can spend time with them."

"Okay. I'll get started on the yard while you're gone." He went to the sink to rinse out his bowl. He glanced at the calendar where he'd been crossing off the days until he would regain his privileges. He gulped, then asked, "Am I still grounded?"

"I'd like to say that your grounding is over—especially since you were so thoughtful in choosing to get milk for my cereal, instead of spending your quarter on an ice cream bar—but I think it's best if you serve your full grounding. Then, maybe next time you will give more thought to your behavior before you act foolishly." She took a last bite of her breakfast and held out her bowl toward Marcus. "I'm running late. Would you mind rinsing this out for me?"

As he tidied up the kitchen, his heart pounded. Why was he even considering disobeying Mama? His first grounding wasn't even over yet, and the next one would be even worse.

Simon was standing in his front yard talking to Patrick when Marcus walked across the gravel to join them. Both boys were holding fishing rods and tackle boxes.

"Are we going fishing?" Marcus asked, his eyes brightening.

"Patrick and I are going fishing in the canal. *You* are going to do my chores while I'm gone." Simon sneered, then chuckled as he motioned for Marcus to follow him through his back gate and into the yard. "I'll expect you to get all these weeds pulled and into those sacks while we're gone. You'd better hustle, too, cause my parents will be back around noon."

Marcus scanned the yard. *So, this is the initiation?* Weeds knee-high dotted the entire landscape. "But, Simon—"

Simon raised his fist even with Marcus's chin. "What did you say, punk?"

Marcus flinched and took a step back. "Nothing."

"When you're done, lean that ladder against the palm tree and pick the dates from it. Be sure you get every last one. Here's the basket. Do a good job and just maybe you can go with us next Saturday—when you're a full-fledged member." Simon walked out the gate and draped his arm around Patrick's shoulders. They walked down the block, turned the corner and were soon out of sight.

Marcus ran his fingers through his hair. He was already sweating in the morning sun. He could feel it burning into his white arms—the curse of being a redhead, Mama always said. He picked up a bag and headed toward the weeds. He wondered if he'd have any energy left to do his own chores when he finished Simon's. As he worked, he daydreamed of Simon's approving nod when Marcus pulled a wriggling fish from the water next week.

Marcus dropped the last of the dates into the basket and placed it next to the six bags of weeds. He turned on the hose and let the cool water run over his head, like he'd been doing all morning. He filled his cupped hands with water and splashed it onto his face. He took a long drink before he turned off the spigot and closed the gate.

Heading toward home, he froze mid-stride when a carload of girls pulled in front of Simon's house. Jennifer Allen was behind the wheel and Sally Schwartz sat beside her. Two girls he didn't know were in the back. He gasped with surprise when Sally gave him a playful grin. He cleared his throat, not knowing whether he should say hello, or not.

"Hi, Marcus." Sally waved him over to the car. "Is Simon home?"

"He and Patrick went fishing." Marcus pointed in the direction of the eastern canal running between the subdivision and the public park. "It's just a couple of blocks away."

"So, what are you doing here?" Jennifer asked, the fingers of one hand looping around a long blonde lock of hair and twirling it over and over again.

"Uh, helping out a little. I just live next door." Marcus could feel the heat rising up his neck and onto his already sunburned cheeks.

The carload of girls turned their heads in the direction of his home and nodded.

"I like the color—pink, like my room." Sally wiggled both hands in his direction. "My favorite. See?"

Marcus cocked his head as he noticed her pink fingernails, pink sweater, and the matching bow in her hair. "Mom likes pink, too."

"Just what do you think you're doing?" Simon called, hurrying down the sidewalk toward them.

Patrick rushed to catch up, carrying a wire basket of crawdads. "Now, calm down, Simon. Don't go all ballistic."

Marcus stepped aside, allowing Simon space next to the car.

But Simon didn't stop. He came straight at him, raised his fist, and punched him square in the face. "That'll teach you to talk to my girl."

The loud crack was followed by girls screaming.

Marcus reacted with a wordless cry of pain. He shook his head, blinked, and then used the corner of his damp T-shirt to catch the first of the blood.

Chapter Four

Pulling the last of the weeds from the front yard planter, Marcus swiped at the sweat streaming onto his swollen face. Mama would be home soon, and he wasn't even close to getting his own chores done. He felt terrible to have gone behind her back. He'd done all that work at Simon's house just to get into his club and all he was probably going to have to show for it was a broken nose and two black eyes. *How will I explain my appearance to Mama?*

"Getting a late start on that yard, aren't you, boy? It's almost one o'clock." Mr. Wilson's head hung out the car window as he pulled into his driveway.

"No, sir. Just had a lot to do. I—"

Simon's father exited the car, opened the door for Simon's mother, and then walked toward Marcus. "What happened to you? Hope you got a good shot back at the other guy." He swung both fists around in front of his body, shadow boxing a few punches into the midday air.

Marcus hung his head. Would he say that if he knew Simon was the "other" guy?

"Just what I thought. There's probably not a mark on him. Better toughen up, Marcus, if you want to make it in this world." He spit onto the sidewalk between them. "I'll make a list of some jobs for you to do around my place. I'll keep track, so we'll know when you've paid off your debt for my broken car window. That is, unless you've got the cash."

Marcus shook his head.

"I didn't think so." Mr. Wilson turned toward his wife. "Go on in, Betty. I'm going to see how Simon's doing in the back yard."

Marcus tossed a handful of weeds into the garbage can and then headed for the shade on the side of the house. He was grounded and now he had to pay Mr. Wilson back, too. Life couldn't get much worse. It was just one more thing to disappoint Mama. She deserved a better son than he was turning out to be.

He stiffened as a loud thud, followed by a series of blood-curdling screams, came from behind the gate to Simon's back yard. A door slammed, followed by muffled yelling coming from inside the Wilsons' house. He could hear both Simon's and his father's raised voices. Was that glass breaking?

Whimpering followed a high-pitched yelp.

Finally, silence.

In the time it took for Marcus to put the gardening tools away and shower, someone had left in the Wilsons' car. He sat by his bedroom window the rest of the afternoon, looking at his baseball card collection and watching for any clue as to what had happened next door.

Mama had pulled into the driveway shortly after one o'clock and had gone directly to her room and shut the door. She needed relief from the sunlight in order to shake the effects of yet another migraine. He'd fix them some soup later. That always seemed to comfort her after she woke.

As the sun dipped beyond the swings of the playground across the street, Marcus watched a lone figure dart across the sidewalk. The person crept up Marcus's driveway and followed the line of steppingstones to where they stopped—under his own bedroom window. Simon's face popped up in front of his own, eyes darting back and forth like a madman. He motioned for Marcus to raise the window.

Marcus shook his head. Simon's nose appeared a bit crooked. Dried blood was smeared across his face. When he opened his mouth to speak, Marcus saw that one of Simon's teeth was missing.

Simon pressed his face to the window, lips forming a ghastly grin, and yelled. "I'll break the window if I have to."

Marcus sighed, then slid the lock to the side and pushed the window up. He stared at Simon, his heart heavy for him, despite the fact that only a few hours earlier he had been on the receiving end of Simon's wrath. "Did your dad do that to you?"

Simon's hand shot through the window, taking hold of his shirt and pulling his head toward him. His body was halfway out the window when he heard Mama's stern voice behind him.

"Marcus! What in the world is going on?"

When Simon let go, Marcus dropped back inside and onto the floor. "Ow!"

"Shut that window, son. If you were headed outside, there's a much easier way. It's called a door." His mother squinted her eyes, peering across the darkened room toward the window.

He blew out a calming breath. Mama hadn't seen Simon. Good. There'd be less explaining to do. "No. Um…I just thought I saw something and I—"

"Come help me with dinner. Maybe if I eat something I can get rid of what's left of this headache." She padded off down the hall; then turned on the kitchen light. Pans rattled, then the sound of the can opener signaled it was soup for dinner, just as he'd predicted.

"I'll be right there."

As he turned back toward the window, Simon's head appeared from the darkness once again. "You're going to look a lot worse than this when I finish with you," he whispered through clenched teeth. "You left the hose out and Dad tripped over it. His foot's broken. Mama took him to the hospital. He beat *me* for something *you* did. I didn't snitch on you, though, because then I'd have to explain what you were doing in our back yard."

"Marcus." Mama's impatient voice only added to the pounding of his heart.

Simon backed away from the window, pointing his finger toward Marcus. "You're a dead man."

Marcus pulled the frame shut and flipped the lock into place. "Coming." He rounded the corner. The smell of vegetable soup filled the air followed by cheese burning in the skillet.

Mama glanced over her shoulder as he entered the room. "It'll just be a minute. I thought grilled cheese sandwiches would taste good for some reason. Soup and sandwiches. Just like at the diner. Can you set the table?"

He pulled out the silverware drawer, took out two spoons and laid them next to the steaming bowls of soup already on the table. His eyes avoided hers as he filled glasses with water from the faucet and placed them beside the bowls.

He took a seat, focusing on the yellow flowers scattered across the thick plastic tablecloth.

"Here you go. Crispy around the edges, just like you like them." Mama placed the gooey sandwich on a small plate to the left of the bowl. "We had some extra bread and cheese left at the end of my shift. Larry said I could have it. Careful not to burn your mouth."

Once Mama was settled at the table next to him, Marcus bowed his head and reached over to take her hand in his, waiting for her to bless the food. How long would he be able to keep her from noticing his face? If he just kept his head down, maybe...

"Lord, we thank you for watching over us and for the unexpected blessing of a pint of milk. We trust you to provide for our needs, no matter how that might happen. Thank you for Marcus. Please watch over Lincoln, wherever he may be."

Marcus huddled over his bowl and dipped his spoon into the broth. He'd worked right through lunch, only now realizing just how hungry he'd become.

"Maybe we can watch a television show or work on our puzzle after dinner."

"I think I'll just go to bed early," Marcus answered between bites of his sandwich.

"You never go to bed early. Don't you feel well?" She reached over to place the back of her hand against his forehead.

"I'm just tired." He tore off a piece of crust, stuffed the last of his sandwich in his mouth and threw the treat to Baxter.

Baxter trotted alongside him as he took his bowl to the sink. He stood on his hind legs, begging for another morsel.

Marcus bent over to rub his ears. "Sorry, boy. You'll have to eat from your own bowl if you're still hungry."

Mama gasped, her hand splayed across her chest. "Marcus, look at me."

He'd almost gotten away with it. Now what? He clenched his teeth together as he slowly turned in her direction.

"Oh, my goodness." Her hand covered her mouth. In an instant, her eyes filled with tears. "What happened to you?"

"I—I—got in a—a—fight."

"With who?"

"It doesn't matter."

"Maybe not to you, but it matters to me." Mama stood and crossed the floor to join him at the sink. She gently ran her fingertips across his nose, cheeks, and lips. "Please, son, answer me."

He started to open his mouth, but shut it quickly. If he told on Simon, things might get even worse...

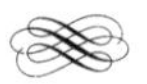

Marcus punched his pillow, making a hollow spot in the center for his head. He lay back, settling into its softness. His eyelids, heavy with sleep, fluttered closed.

Suddenly, strong arms yanked him from his bike and shoved something over his head. His struggles were useless against the strength of his kidnappers… killers? His mind raced to make sense of it all. Maybe they were aliens…

They dragged him along the sidewalk—then across gravel—and finally onto the grass. A door creaked open. He was shoved forward. The door shut behind him with a bang, footsteps retreating across the gravel and into the distance.

He yanked the covering off his head, expelling a sigh of relief. His eyes traveled through the darkness, focusing on narrow shafts of light that filtered in between jagged boards. He brought his face up close and peered outside. Cactus. He could see nothing but cactus.

He fell back against the roughness of a wall and slid down to the dirt floor. As his eyes adjusted to the darkness, he gasped. He had landed on a narrow ledge. Beyond it, a deep cavern belched up a putrid smell. He scrambled back to the door, pushing against it with all his might. When it failed to budge, he began to scream. "Help!" Please, let someone find me.

Something fluttered up from below, hitting the side of his head. He swatted it away with his hands, pulling back as sharp teeth bit into his thumb. The odd, high-pitched chirping called more of its kind. Soon the entire space was filled with wings, flapping all around him and crying out in unison.

He tucked his head down and covered his ears with his hands.

Celia dried the frying pan with the thin kitchen towel and placed it into the bottom cupboard. She grabbed the prescription bottle from the Lazy Susan and let the last capsule drop into her hand. She inspected the label. One more refill. She'd call the pharmacy tomorrow.

She walked to the living room window overlooking the driveway and peered out just as the streetlights switched on. Whoever had been outside earlier was sure to be gone now. She put her forehead against the coolness of the glass and closed her eyes. Why was Marcus being so stubborn? Why wouldn't he tell her the name of the kid he'd fought with? Fear. That was the only answer. He was afraid the boy would retaliate.

She slid into the rocking chair she'd inherited from her mother, resting her head back against its high wooden back. It had proven to be her best thinking place, just as it had been her mother's. The thoughts of her rocking and knitting were comforting. The vision of her hands, gnarled with rheumatoid arthritis, had translated into words in Celia's memory. They said, "*Keep on going. Don't let anything or anyone defeat you.*"

No, she wouldn't give up. Not on Marcus. Not on herself. Not on her dead-end job. For as long as she could, she'd believe the best about those she loved—even Lincoln. Wherever he was, whatever he was doing, she hoped he'd feel her prayers and somehow find his way back to his family—back to the son who was certain to need him when...

She shook her head from her morbid thoughts. It would do her no good to travel down that path—the future would be what the future would be. Instead, she'd consider what should be done about Marcus. *More punishment?* His teenage years had crept up on them, causing her sleepless nights and days spent worrying that she'd somehow failed him—and just what, if anything, she could do about it.

The minute hand on the cuckoo clock clicked as it reached the hour. Its door opened, the crudely-carved bird rushing out to crow eight times. She poured herself a glass of lemonade and carried it outside to the porch. She reached back inside for a cushion, placing it beneath her on the concrete steps.

There was a full moon tonight. It was a perfect evening for the boys to play baseball. She guessed, however, that it being Saturday night, they were out with dates or maybe a sporting event. She looked back toward the house and Marcus's dark bedroom window. *Except for her son.*

She took a long sip of lemonade and was just about to go down memory lane for the millionth time—reliving the birth of her son and the stinging words Lincoln had said when he left—when Simon rounded the corner. She watched as moonlight and streetlight combined forces to perfectly illuminate his face—cut lip, bruised cheeks, and one eye swollen halfway shut.

He limped toward the folded evening newspaper lying on the sidewalk, visibly wincing as he bent over and picked it up.

Looks like he's been in a fight… She felt herself go limp. She put her head between her knees and took deep calming breaths.

Surely Marcus was not capable of doing something like this…

Marcus woke with a start, panting and shivering as the bedside fan blew air over his sweaty head and arms. He swung his feet over the side of the bed and ran to flip the wall switch, turning on the overhead light. He looked around the bedroom and blew out several breaths as he oriented himself back to the present. No bats. He laughed nervously. It had only been a dream.

He ran his fingers through his hair, willed his breathing to slow down, and headed toward the kitchen for a drink of water. En route, he slapped his cheeks with the palms of his hands. *Wake up, Marcus.* There was only one explanation for a dream like that—he was in danger.

The glass was empty when he placed it back onto the counter. Tears ran down his cheeks as he hugged himself and shook his head from side to side. What could he do?

"Marcus."

He turned in the direction of Mama's voice. He blinked. Her eyes were red and puffy. No doubt he'd been the reason for her crying.

"We need to talk."

Chapter Five

Marcus hadn't seen Simon at school, nor around the neighborhood, all week long. Mr. Wilson's Oldsmobile remained parked in the driveway, dust and dirt accumulating on his pride and joy over the past few days.

Marcus could do nothing but watch and wait. His grounding had been extended a week. He told Mama it wasn't fair—that he wasn't guilty of causing Simon's injuries—but she was certain punishment was in order.

He slid open the closet door, staring at his Spider-Man costume on the top shelf. He looked ahead to Saturday, when he would once again have television privileges. He'd wear the costume while lying on the sofa, eating popcorn and watching his movie. The grounding would soon be a thing of the past.

A sharp knock on the front door drew him away from the closet. He meandered down the hall and pushed back the curtain to see Frannie, Mama's friend from the diner, standing outside. He watched her for a moment, as she smoothed the skirt of her uniform, then rocked back and forth—heel to toe—as she waited for him to answer the door.

He swung it open, pasting on a big smile. "Hi, Frannie."

"Hi, Marcus. May I come in?" She placed a soggy tissue in her pocket.

He stepped backward. "Sure. Mama's not home, though."

"I know. That's what I want to talk to you about." She walked past him and sat down gently on the worn sofa, patting the space beside her. "Come and sit. I want to tell you what happened at work today."

Marcus could feel his throat and chest tighten. All of a sudden, he couldn't breathe. Mama wasn't here. Instead, Frannie had come. He slumped down next to her, turning sideways to look deep into her hazel eyes. Something was wrong.

She placed her hand on top of his. "Your Mama wasn't feeling well at work this afternoon. We called an ambulance to take her to the hospital. She's going to rest there tonight, and have some tests done tomorrow."

Marcus sucked in a deep breath and let it out, slowly. "Mama's not coming home?"

"Not tonight, I'm afraid, Marcus. Unfortunately, visiting hours are over, or I'd take you by to see her. You're welcome to come home with me, if you'd like. We have a guest room you can stay in. We live near the diner, you know."

"I know, but I can stay by myself. I'll be okay." He reached for Baxter, stroking the dog's fur as he continued to sleep on his pillow at the end of the sofa. "I have my dog to keep me company."

"That's what your Mama said." Frannie bent over to give Baxter a pat on the back and then slipped a piece of paper next to the phone in the kitchen. "She said she'd give me time to get over here and talk to you and then she'd be calling you later. I'd better be getting home. I left my phone number. Be sure to call me if you need anything. Okay?"

Marcus followed her to the door. "Frannie?"

She turned back in his direction. "Yes?"

He stared at her for a moment, and then replied. "Oh, nothing."

Once she'd gone, he felt more alone than he could ever remember. He hugged himself against a sudden shiver, contemplating the question he'd not dared to ask Frannie. *Will Mama die?*

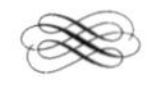

Celia pulled the sheet up over her shoulders. The orderly had still not returned with the additional blanket she had requested more than an hour ago. Maybe he'd forgotten, or there'd been an emergency…

She stared at the metal railings on the sides of the hospital bed. The nurse had assured her they were there for her protection, in case she felt dizzy. Perhaps the tests would reveal whether the stroke had been a sign of her disease or if it was completely unrelated.

She pulled her reading glasses down from the top of her head and perched them on her nose. Then she reached for her purse and extracted her wallet. The zipper stuck, as usual, but she soon wiggled it free.

She pulled out several photos from the side pocket, studying them one at a time.

The first picture was of Mama and Papa, standing in front of the chicken coop. It had been Mama's birthday and Papa had got her—of all things—more baby chicks. Thinking it was a joke of some kind, Celia had later looked around for a package on the sideboard. But there wasn't one. Papa loved his chickens and he figured everyone appreciated them as much as he did. No matter that Mama had been eyeing a cornflower blue shawl from the Penny's catalog.

The next picture was of Celia and Lincoln, taken the day they got married. Her dress was simple—three-quarter length sleeves and a scooped neck—covered in white eyelet. The color was very important in those days—a not-so-subtle way of confirming the bride's virginity.

The last picture, taken by her father when he and Mama had come to visit Celia in the hospital after Marcus's birth, captured Celia's jubilant smile. It gave no hint of her baby's condition or the fact that her husband had walked out on her only hours earlier.

When Frannie poked her head around the curtain separating Celia's bed from that of her roommate, she looked up with a wide grin, pleased to have a visitor. She slid the pictures underneath the crisp, white sheet, keeping them—just like her memories—to herself.

Frannie slipped into the straight-backed vinyl chair beside the bed. "How are you feeling? Better, I hope."

"A little tired, I guess. I miss being at home."

"That's understandable. But I came by to let you know that I talked with Marcus and he sends his love. He's looking forward to your phone call."

Celia raised her eyebrows. "He wasn't too upset about me not coming home?"

"A little, of course, but when I told him that he was welcome at our home, he said he'd be fine there by himself. I haven't really been around him enough to know how much he really understands about things."

Celia could feel her face getting hot. "I wish people would learn that while Marcus may *look* different than other children, he's still of average intelligence. He understands most things any other seventeen-year-old boy would. To be sure, though, he's grown up to be a little reserved because of the way he's always been avoided by other children—and their parents."

Frannie's eyes grew wide. She twisted the hem of her skirt in her hands. "Sorry. I've probably drawn conclusions that I shouldn't have."

Celia gave Frannie's hand a gentle squeeze. "No offense taken. I even find myself reacting that way, sometimes. It's like he's one person on the outside and quite another on the inside. It's his lack of social skills that makes it hard for others to see him for who he really is."

"Well, thanks for understanding." Frannie stood and stretched. "It's been a long day, so I'd best be getting along home. Besides, the nurse gave me strict orders to only stay a few minutes. Have someone from the hospital give me a call when you get discharged and I'll come over and drive you home."

As the door closed behind her friend, Celia found herself saying a silent prayer for her boy, beseeching God for his safety until she returned. She reached under the sheet, brought out his picture and studied it for a moment before reaching for the phone.

It was dark when Marcus woke with a start. He'd filled up on popcorn, then fallen asleep on the sofa after his brief talk with Mama. He had relaxed once he heard her voice and she had assured him that she would be coming home tomorrow.

He stared at the empty popcorn bowl. He had broken the terms of his punishment, but he hoped Mama would forgive him, under the circumstances. He reached to turn on the light, but he froze when he heard a noise coming from the direction of his bedroom. His hands shook as he picked up his baseball bat from the corner. He felt his way down the familiar hallway, his knees knocking as he crept closer to the open door.

The beam from a flashlight zigzagged across the room, casting eerie shadows. *A burglar!* Marcus peered between the door and its frame, watching as a guy dressed in black took something from the top shelf of the closet. The package crinkled as he stuffed it inside his jacket and ran the zipper upward. Turning toward the door, the light revealed the face he'd come to know so well.

Marcus pushed the door the rest of the way open with the palm of his hand. "What are you doing, Simon?"

"I—I just came to get Colin's package." Simon took a step backward. "Look, if you don't believe me." He pulled the brown bag out from under his jacket.

Marcus raised his eyebrows. "Why didn't you just ask me for it?"

"I thought you'd be at the hospital. Frannie told my mother what happened."

Both boys jumped at the sudden sound of the doorbell ringing. Simon was the first to move. He ran to the bedroom window and peeked out the curtains, as they fluttered in the night air. "It's the police."

Marcus looked around the corner toward the entry door. "I'll be right back." He wondered what they could want in the middle of the night. They should know people would be asleep at this hour. He unlocked the door and opened it a crack. "What do you want?"

An officer, somewhat familiar in appearance, brought his face up toward him. "Hello, Marcus. Remember me? Officer Franklin from Halloween?"

He opened the door a little wider. "Sure."

"Your mother asked for a patrol of your house this evening, in case there was any trouble, or you needed anything. When we saw the light on, we decided to see if you were all right."

His stomach flip-flopped. "I—I'm fine, o—officer."

At the sound of scuffling, officer Franklin stepped back. Another patrolman rounded the corner, pushing Simon forward to join them on the porch.

"Caught this one sneaking out of the bedroom window." He took the package from Simon and held it out, toward Marcus. "This yours, son?"

"I, um… not exactly." Marcus looked to Simon for direction. He pressed his lips together, remembering Simon's earlier admonition not to tell.

Simon glared at him, his fists clenched. "Come on, now, Marcus. These are policemen you're talking to. They can see right through you. They know it belongs to you." He paused; then turned to the officers. "It's his.

He shoved it into my hands when you rang the bell. He told me to jump out the window and get rid of it."

Marcus balled his fingers into a fist. He stared down Simon, but he remained silent.

The officer put the package up to his ear and shook it. "So, what do we think is in this little brown bag? Jewelry? A bottle of perfume, perhaps? Oh, I know, how about a little 'weed'?" Officer Franklin's lip curled, revealing a gleaming gold tooth. He jammed the point of his pencil into the paper, tearing a quarter-sized hole in it. Out spilled tender green leaves. "Just as I suspected, Brian. We've got ourselves two little drug runners."

Marcus could feel his face and neck turning red. "That can't be true. It's a present for Colin's girlfriend. I've been keeping it for him until her birthday."

"Who's this Colin?" The officer tapped his pencil against his leather notebook.

Marcus shook his head, running his fingers through his matted hair. "I don't know his last name."

"Do you know where he lives?"

"No." Marcus wiped his sweaty palms across his T-shirt.

The officer raised his eyebrows. "He's a friend of yours, isn't he?"

"No."

"You mean to tell us you kept a package in your home for a guy you don't even know?" The officer sucked air in through his teeth, then spit on Mama's favorite rose bush.

Marcus took a step back, keeping his eyes glued to the bush. He didn't appreciate him disrespecting Mama, but he decided to let it go. The officer wouldn't care to hear the story of how it came to be planted there… "Simon said to. We all do what Simon says."

The officers looked at each other and broke out laughing.

"You're kidding us, right?" the plump officer asked, doubling over with laughter.

Marcus wrinkled his brow. "No, I'm not."

"Well, now doesn't that just beat all, Franklin?"

"I've never heard an excuse like that before."

"Since you are blaming each other, we have no choice but to take both of you in for further questioning. We'll bring this Colin kid in, too, as soon as we can. Get his side of the story."

"Are—are we un—under arrest?" Marcus sputtered.

"For right now, we're just taking you in for questioning. But if we find out you're selling 'weed' to kids in your school or the neighborhood, we can most certainly arrest you."

"Look what trouble you've gotten us into, now, Marcus." Simon sneered as the officer shoved him toward the cruiser.

Marcus felt tears well in his eyes and a lump form in his throat. Once he was seated in the backseat of the squad car next to Simon, he leaned forward, cradling his head in his hands. *Why won't they believe me?*

"I'll secure the premises." Officer Bruce walked toward the house.

Marcus watched as the lights went out, room by room. He had to convince them that he was innocent—at least of the stealing part. He'd been tempted, several times, to take a look in the package, himself, but had never gotten up enough nerve to do it. Strange, though, why would Colin want to give his girlfriend weeds for her birthday?"

Celia paced back and forth, from the kitchen to the living room and back again, waiting for Marcus to return home. Just as she had been unlocking the door, earlier that afternoon, she had rushed to the ringing telephone. If she had known it would be the police department, informing her of her son's whereabouts—jail, of all places—she wouldn't have answered it.

Her already-high blood pressure and weakened heart would be in worse shape than ever until this latest ordeal was over. She drew the kitchen's checkered café curtain back, observing the backyard grill and picnic table they rarely used.

She returned to the living room. The pillow and blanket from Marcus's bed were lying on the sofa. She retrieved a bowl with a handful of popcorn kernels, which was perched precariously on the edge of the coffee table. *Another punishment unheeded. Why was he becoming so defiant?* She folded the blanket and placed it on the end of the sofa, then sat down.

Her hands stroked Baxter's soft fur. He was already over 100 years old—in people years, of course—and slept most of the time. However, his presence was still comforting to both her and Marcus.

Her fingers played with a loose thread on one of the cushions. It would be Thanksgiving tomorrow. She had a turkey breast in the freezer, but no energy—or inclination, really—to cook. At the moment, she felt very little to be thankful for this year. Marcus's behavior was getting out of control and her heart was giving out. She was fearful as to just what this latest round of tests would show.

She was drying her eyes when two cruisers pulled up—one into her driveway, the other into the Wilsons'. She took a deep breath.

Simon's influence was at the heart of it all.

Chapter Six

On Monday of the following week, Marcus and Mama left the courtroom mid-afternoon. The sun was at its brightest, but the skyscrapers in downtown Phoenix blocked out most of its rays. An unexpected breeze played with the hem of Mama's skirt, causing her to blush in the presence of a sidewalk filled with passing strangers.

They walked two blocks to the parking lot and waited in the car a full five minutes before another motorist stopped to let them back out. "This is what they call 'rush hour' in Phoenix, son. I'm glad we don't have to fight this every day."

Marcus nodded. He wasn't thinking about traffic, though. He was already replaying the hearing in his mind—the judge's stern reprimand, Simon's scowl from across the room, and the sharp whack of the gavel.

Marcus had spent several sleepless nights worrying about how to answer the questions that would be put to him, but he had fretted needlessly. He had not been called to testify. Instead, someone read his statement into the record—to save time, he guessed.

He cleared his throat as Mama stopped at yet another red light. "Mama, am I going to go to jail?"

She shook her head. "No. The judge sentenced you and Simon to community service. But since Colin is nineteen, he'll have a full-fledged trial."

"What's community service?" The judge must have explained it, but his knees had been knocking and his hands shaking so badly, Marcus couldn't focus on his words. Now, alone in the car with Mama, the details of his punishment loomed foremost on his mind.

"It means just what it says. You'll have to do jobs—chores, if you will—in the community. They could be picking up trash, volunteering at the hospital, sweeping off sidewalks. Any number of things, really, for two hours after school each day and half-days on Saturdays for ninety days." The car lurched forward as the light turned green.

"The judge didn't even listen to my story."

"He heard your testimony as it was read. It included everything—the part about how you came to have the package…the fact that you didn't know what was inside the wrapping…the promise you made to Simon. It was all there. And I think he believed you. It's just that he wants to teach you boys a lesson. He's trying to make an impression on you so that you think twice before you ever do anything like this again."

"But, Mama—"

"Marcus, you need to face up to your consequences. I hope you learn from it, so you'll give more thought to your actions in the future." She cut the conversation short. "It's been a long afternoon for both of us. I'd like to do some thinking and praying for the next few minutes, if you don't mind." She focused her attention back on the road, her thoughts a mystery to all but God.

Marcus leaned back against the headrest, lost in the melodies as Mama's gospel music played softly on the radio. His eyelids, heavy from a restless sleep the night before, fluttered shut to the sound of "I Come to The Garden Alone."

Moments later—or at least it seemed like that—Marcus shivered as he woke. He was up to his neck in smelly water. Late afternoon shadows fell across the bank of a canal. *What's happening? We headed for home...* "Mama! Mama!"

He grabbed onto the steering wheel as he fought against the swift current. Waves of water pushed him up onto the dashboard, pinning him against the windshield. He floated on his back with only a few inches of air separating the incoming water from the roof of the car. He gulped in what little air he could and submerged himself, swimming underwater. He had to find her. *God, please help...*

As if in answer, an arm flopped against his shoulder.

Mama! His lungs were burning for air, but he put his hands under her arms and started pulling. Water stung his nose and he pressed his lips tight to keep from swallowing it. He fought against the rushing torrent with all his might.

With a loud splash, someone jumped into the water. "Hold on, kid, let me help you." A bald-headed guy with thick glasses and muscular arms reached through the open window and helped him drag Mama's wet, heavy body, inch by inch, out of the car and up the embankment.

Marcus's teeth chattered, and his breath came in raspy gasps as they laid her onto the dirt path alongside the canal. When he heard the sound of people cheering, he looked up. Cars had parked along the side of the road and a crowd of gawkers had gathered. He collapsed in the dirt and then rolled onto his back to catch his breath.

An ambulance screeched to a halt. Two men in white coats ran toward them. One placed a warm blanket around Marcus's shoulders, the other dropped to his knees and turned Mama onto her back. He pressed on her chest, over and over again.

The onlookers clapped when Mama sputtered, coughed, and opened her eyes. Several of them gave Marcus a thumbs-up.

They wasted no time in placing Mama on a stretcher and rushing her inside the open double doors. Marcus followed on foot, using his last ounce of energy to hoist himself into the back of the vehicle. As he massaged her lifeless hand, he looked through the back window and mouthed a silent *thank you* to the man who had helped him rescue Mama from the water.

As the siren blared and tires squealed, he laid his head on the pillow next to hers and wept.

After spending the night with Mama at the hospital, Marcus went home to shower. He slept the rest of the morning; then headed to school after lunch.

At four o'clock, he joined Simon for their orientation with Mrs. Samuelson, a social worker assigned to their case by the court. He'd been nervous about his first day of community service, but today he was actually thankful to have something to do besides sit in the hospital waiting room and worry about Mama.

Mrs. Samuelson relayed good news from the hospital and then dropped them off at a city park in Tempe where they were told to clean both public restrooms. Normally, he would have cringed at scrubbing toilets and dirty restroom floors, but nothing could put a damper on his feelings of happiness today. He danced around the mop bucket as he pushed it down the sidewalk. Mama was alive. God had answered his prayers.

The park was nearly deserted when Marcus finished cleaning the half-dozen sinks and toilets in the ladies' restroom. Simon was flat on his back atop a nearby picnic table, his ball cap shielding his closed eyes, when Marcus emerged from the open door. He walked over and poked Simon's shoulder. "You done already?"

Simon stretched as he woke. "Huh?"

"Are you finished?" Marcus nodded in the direction of the men's restroom.

"Of course not. You'd better hustle so we can get out of here before dark."

"Me? The women's restroom is clean as a whistle." Marcus sighed, glad to have that miserable duty behind him.

"Good for you. You're halfway there." Simon's stony expression could only mean trouble.

"No, the men's restroom is *your* job."

"You want to test me? 'Cause I'll be happy to tell Colin who it was that snitched on him. Once he knows it was you that earned him a stint in the slammer, he'll be counting the days until he gets out. When he hunts you down, you'll wish you had some protection. I'll enjoy standing by and watching you squirm. Remember, no work, no help."

Marcus covered his ears to drown out Simon's laughter. Would his unfair treatment ever end? Simon would never learn his lesson if Marcus gave in to him. Still, it was clear that he'd need someone to defend him against Colin. *There's no other choice.*

Marcus pulled the mop bucket in the direction of the men's restroom. He looked back over his shoulder, glaring at Simon who was already asleep and probably dreaming of Sally Schwartz. *She's a nice girl. How long will it be until she sees Simon for who he really is?*

There were four urinals on the wall separating the men's and women's restrooms—and two disgusting toilets. When Marcus flushed the last one, the water started to go down, but came back up with a vengeance. It overflowed raw sewage onto the floor. He held his nose and tried not to gag.

He wiggled the handle, but the smelly brown muck kept flowing out, non-stop. It billowed forth like lava from a volcano. On and on it came, running out the door and onto the sidewalk. Unable to stop the relentless flow, Marcus ran to the door.

"Help!"

Day two of community service couldn't be any worse than the first. Marcus dug the toe of his still-damp tennis shoe into the soft dirt in front of Resurrection Community Church's double glass doors as he waited for Pastor Brice Grayson. He folded the sheet of paper with his assignment on it written in big, bold letters and stuffed it into the pocket of his windbreaker. He couldn't imagine what kind of help the church would need—or that he'd be qualified to give.

Most of his life, Marcus had attended services with his mother, but as he had approached his teenage years, he'd balked at going. She wasn't one to give up easily, though, so they had compromised. She sat near the front where she could see and hear everything; Marcus occupied a seat in the back, doodling or snoozing away the one hour and fifteen minutes of worship time before escaping out the side door when the last hymn ended.

Up until the accident, God had seemed like a distant being—someone living above the clouds—sitting on his throne doing whatever gods do. Marcus had thought of Him as someone who looked down on earth, occasionally, to see how people were behaving. Like, perhaps, on Easter and Christmas, or in times of disaster.

"Hello, Marcus." The pastor's eyes sparkled behind his wire-rimmed glasses. He gave Marcus a pat on the back. "It's been a long time since I've seen you, young man. I hear you're to give me some help around here on Mondays. Is that right?"

Marcus stood, hands shaking, and took a deep breath. *Here goes…* "Y-yes, sir."

"No reason to be nervous, son. I won't bite." He pushed back his straw hat, revealing a receding hairline. He chuckled good-naturedly.

"I guess not. You've always seemed friendly enough."

"Well, you seem nice, too, so I guess we can both relax and get to know each other." He motioned for Marcus to follow him around the side of the brick building and into a small flower garden bridging the gap between the church and the gas station on the corner. "Let's sit over here in the shade and talk a bit." The pastor removed his hat and wiped his forehead with a handkerchief.

Marcus followed the pastor, pushing past overgrown vines and tromping over fallen leaves that crunched under his feet. They came to a clearing where two stone benches faced each other. Beyond them, several rose bushes surrounded an empty water fountain with angels of various sizes perched on its rim.

Pastor Brice brushed dried leaves from both benches and then motioned for Marcus to sit. "Sorry state of affairs, this garden. I don't think anyone's been out here for six months or more. But that should soon change. Your mother has told me you are quite the gardener—good with plants and all."

"Yeah. I like doing yard work, except when it's so hot outside." He sat on the hard bench closest to the trellis that must have once been filled with cascading vines. From the appearance of the dried branches, he guessed they had been honeysuckle. He closed his eyes for a brief moment, drinking in the faint fragrance that, remarkably, still lingered. Its reminder of Mama's favorite perfume brought unexpected tears to his eyes.

"Thinking about your mother?" Pastor Brice scrounged in his pocket and produced another handkerchief. He held it out toward Marcus.

Marcus wiped his eyes and then nodded. "How'd you know?"

"Your case worker called early this morning. She said there was a chance that you wouldn't show, since your mother has been in the hospital."

"They moved her to Crestview. Her heart's under a great strain. It's mostly my fault." Tears streamed down his cheeks unchecked. He used the handkerchief to blow his nose before he continued. "I haven't been the best son, lately." He clamped his hand down on the pastor's. "But, I—I'm gonna do better. Really, I am. God answered my prayer for Mama. He's real, just like she said all along. I know that now."

Pastor Brice patted his arm. "Looks like you and I will do good to get acquainted this week. It will be soon enough, next Monday, to get to the gardening."

Marcus beamed. "That's what you want me to do—yard work?"

"I'd say this prayer garden needs some help, wouldn't you?" The Pastor raised his arm, sweeping over the entire area in one gigantic arc.

"It sure does." Marcus felt his spirits lift. Community service might not be so bad after all. He couldn't believe he'd be working in this beautiful garden every week. He grinned as his eyes met the Pastor's. He could hardly wait to tell Mama the news. It felt like...did he dare say it...that he'd made his first true friend in his whole life?

Seafood. That's what Mama always called it when Marcus ate with his mouth open. He cringed to think what she'd say if she were sitting at this picnic table watching Simon's ham and cheese sandwich go 'round and 'round before he swallowed.

Marcus struggled to keep his mind on the conversation with the social worker and answer her questions. "Mama's at a rehabilitation center. She'll have to stay there until she gets better." His tired eyes met the sparkling blue ones of Mrs. Samuelson. *They're the same shade as Mama's.*

"So, it was her weak heart that caused her to black out and lose control of the car?" She wrote on a notepad as she talked and finished off her French fries. She looked up at Marcus with an encouraging smile.

He nodded. "Until they figure out what to do for her, she'll need plenty of rest and quiet."

"So, you're staying with your mother's friend, Frannie Johnson, right?"

He felt his face grow hot, as he inspected his shoelaces. Was he breaking some law by staying by himself when Mrs. Samuelson had expressly told him to stay at the Johnsons'? He kept his eyes to the ground. "I know you—and Mama—expect me to stay at her house, but I'd rather be at home, sleeping in my own bed. Anyway, Baxter needs to be walked and fed. It just makes more sense for me to go on home after community service each night."

"I do understand your thinking, but the state has other ideas and you're going to have to adhere to their rules. Do I make myself clear?" Her smile-less face revealed just how serious she was. "Now, let's talk about how we are doing so far in our community service. I'd like to know what you boys have learned during your service to the state."

Simon laughed and shook his head. "Only that the judge has got his head on backwards."

Mrs. Samuelson bit her lower lip. "Let's be serious, Simon. Smart remarks will get you nowhere fast—and you may just find yourself doing community service for an extended period of time."

Simon swallowed hard. "Okay. Yeah. This is teaching me that I don't want to have to do community service again. Maybe I'll watch what I do more carefully in the future."

She scribbled on her notepad again. "That's good, Simon. Just what the judge is looking for—and a little remorse wouldn't hurt anything, either." She turned her attention to Marcus.

He shrugged his shoulders. "Mondays are my favorite. I like gardening at the church and the pastor has been teaching me about God. He says Jesus is my friend, same as the pastor is."

Simon spit in the dirt. "What a joke. You can't be serious. Jesus is no friend...least of all yours."

"He said Jesus is willing to be *anyone's* friend. Even yours, Simon." It pained him to speak the words, but the pastor said there was forgiveness even for the worst of sinners...

Simon's nose flared, and his face turned red. "Why would I want Him for a friend? I don't need someone else in my life giving me orders...telling me what a screw-up I am."

Marcus took a deep breath, his answer barely audible. "It's not like that. I—"

"Put a lid on it, Marcus." Simon lunged at him and yanked the collar of his shirt, pulling it so tight that the top button popped off and his dirty fingernails scraped the side of his neck.

"Simon!" Mrs. Samuelson grabbed his arm, looking him straight in the eye.

He gave the shirt collar one last pull before letting him go with a forward push that sent Marcus sprawling onto the gravel. A thin line of blood trickled down the calf of his right leg.

"You just wait, Simon." Marcus grabbed onto the picnic bench and pulled himself to his feet. His heart was pounding. He found it hard to believe Simon didn't want a friend like Jesus.

Mrs. Samuelson retrieved a tissue and a Band Aid from her purse and handed them to Marcus. "Now, gentlemen, this intolerance of each other is the very thing that gets you into trouble. Both of you sit down." She cleared her throat, studied the stack of papers in front of her, and after several tense moments, looked up.

"Marcus, would you be interested in increasing your time doing landscaping and maintenance at the church, if the pastor is agreeable?"

Had he heard right? No more cleaning restrooms? "Sure."

"I think separating you boys would be the best thing all around. Simon, I'm going to put you on city parks four days a week."

Marcus stifled a laugh.

Simon stood up, bringing his fist smashing down on the top of the picnic table. "That's not fair. Picking up trash and cleaning bathrooms is cruel and unusual punishment."

"Somehow, we've got to break your attitude, Simon. Your head is in the toilet, son. In my opinion, this community service is much too light a punishment for an incorrigible young man like you. But I'm not the judge…just the enforcer of his wishes." She took a deep breath and turned back to Marcus. "If you have any free time, our yard is looking pretty sorry. Since my husband hurt his back, he hasn't been able to keep it up very well."

Marcus gulped down the last bite of his sandwich and threw the paper sack into the garbage can. "Sure, Mrs. Samuelson. I can mow and trim for you Saturday afternoon."

"I'm going to report you to the judge, fat lady. You're going easy on Marcus just to get a favor from him. You're about to lose your cushy job. But don't worry. I happen to know there'll soon be an opening at the city park cleaning toilets."

Mrs. Samuelson glared at Simon before placing her hand on Marcus's shoulder. "Simon jumped to conclusions, Marcus. We'd expect to pay you. I'm not asking a favor. I'm offering you a job."

Later that evening, Marcus left his chair by Mama's bedside and walked to the window. He could see the large white cross on the roof of Resurrection Community Church from his mother's hospital room. He thought back to his conversation with Pastor Brice the week before. He had felt so good in his presence, unlike most of the men who had come and gone in his and Mama's lives over the years.

Marcus was different. Everyone knew it. He hadn't blamed any of them for not wanting to be saddled with the responsibility of a boy like him.

The only man he couldn't forgive in his heart was his father. Mama never talked about it, but Marcus knew that he'd left because he couldn't stand to look at him—the gaping hole caused by the cleft lip. He ran his forefinger across the slightly raised and jagged scar formed by a doctor's sutures. There hadn't been enough money for a skilled plastic surgeon…

But Mama had always done her best by him, denying herself new clothes or shoes in order to put food on the table. Throughout the years, she continued to put Marcus first, often working seven days a week—twelve to fourteen-hour days. Her only extravagance was a membership to the Desert Botanical Gardens. *Oh, how she loved desert flowers…*

When the repetitive alarm sounded from a machine at Mama's bedside, he jumped from the chair and grabbed her hand. "No!"

All of a sudden, he was pushed aside by a nurse. As more people in white rushed into the room, he was driven farther and farther from the bedside.

Marcus had become accustomed to the routine efforts to help Mama. Still, he felt his heart begin to pound as he watched from a nearby corner.

Chapter Seven

At the sudden crack of thunder, Baxter hopped onto the foot of the bed.

Marcus reached down to pat the dog's head. "It's just a noise, buddy. Nothing to be scared about." He tried to sound brave, but he had to admit that the noise also bothered him. It always upset Mama, too. Without a closet at the rehab center to hide in—as they usually did at home—he tried to imagine her, now, curled up in her hospital bed with the covers over her head.

He slid into his own closet with his dog, saying a quick prayer of thanks to God for saving Mama one more time. *I know the day will come when you take Mama to Heaven, though. Please help me be brave when you do.*

He was glad he was home with Baxter, even though he'd promised the social worker he'd stay at Frannie's.

He had actually put a change of clothes in his backpack and started over there after supper, but once he saw the dark clouds gathering, he just knew he could never sleep anywhere else except in his own bed. *How can I make Mrs. Samuelson understand?*

When the skies fell silent, Marcus opened the closet door. Crossing the floor, he pulled back the window blinds. The full moon was surrounded by hazy wisps of white. If the rain continued, he wouldn't be mowing tomorrow for Mr. Wilson—and he wouldn't be earning any of the extra money he'd been counting on from Mrs. Samuelson. He crossed his fingers at first, but then shook his head and offered a silent prayer for clear skies. He needed that money to buy Mama's Christmas present.

He was about to let the blinds fall back in place when he noticed Simon's red car rolling backward toward the street. No, Simon was pushing it. Marcus watched as Simon ran forward, reached through the open window, and grabbed onto the steering wheel. He guided the vehicle halfway down the street. Then, as it neared the stop sign, he opened the door and jumped in. As he drove away, Marcus tried to make sense of what he had just witnessed. Was the battery dead, was the car out of gas, or was Simon simply sneaking off without permission?

It rained the rest of the weekend, but by Monday afternoon the sun was shining once more. Pastor Brice nodded his head and scribbled a few notes as Marcus opened up to him about his problems in relating to others—especially to Simon, the neighborhood bully. "I just can't seem to stand up to him, even when I know the things he orders me to do are wrong." He hung his head, watching an army of ants travel across the garden's cobblestone walkway.

"Why do you think you need to follow Simon's commands?"

"'Cause he's Simon. Everybody does what Simon says. You know...Simon Says—"

"Marcus, surely you understand that *Simon Says* is just a game." The pastor tapped his pencil against the palm of his outstretched hand, a cadence mimicking that of the dripping faucet behind the bench where he sat.

Marcus shook his head. "It's not a game. Games are *fun.*"

Pastor Brice chuckled, then leaned over to rest his elbows on his knees. He laced and unlaced his fingers before he spoke. "Son, Simon has you believing he's your boss, but nothing could be further from the truth."

Marcus hung his head, speaking barely above a whisper. "He says if I don't do what he says, there'll be *consequences.*"

"The Bible says, 'If God is for us, who can be against us?' He alone is all powerful."

Marcus smiled ear-to-ear. "You mean he'll stick up for me against Simon?"

"Let's just say that He's against the things Simon is telling you to do. And He's against Simon's threats, too. If you'll be obedient to God, He'll be your champion. He'll work everything out in the end. You just have to trust Him."

Marcus bit his lip. "I don't know..."

"Even though you can't hear or see Him, God *is* real. His Word is true. He won't let you down." Pastor Brice raised his eyebrows. "How about it?"

"Simon's bigger and smarter than me."

"But, there is someone who's bigger and stronger than Simon."

Marcus wiped his eyes with the back of his hand. "God?"

Pastor Brice laughed as he stood and stretched. He looked down at Marcus. "Will you give Him a chance? Let Him show you what He can do?"

"Maybe if I just stay away from Simon..."

The pastor placed his large hand on his shoulder as Marcus fell in step with him. "That might work for a while, but eventually you'll run into each other again. And when you do, I'm thinking you'll want someone in your corner. Am I right?"

The following week, when her insurance ran out, Celia was discharged from Crestview. She had no choice but to come home. In reality, it was where she wanted to be, but she knew she needed more care... And getting back to work was a necessity. However, she knew that was impossible. Goodness, she couldn't even walk to the bathroom and back without assistance.

From her bed, she heard the front door open.

"Yoo-hoo," Frannie called from the kitchen. "I'm just going to heat this soup up for you and then I'll come in for a short visit."

Celia strained to push herself up in bed. On the third attempt, she managed to wedge a pillow behind her back. "Make it a small bowl." *I haven't had much of an appetite...*

"Oh, you'll like it. Larry made it himself. I think the old grouch misses you."

Larry had recently invited Celia to a movie and dinner. He'd been sweet on her for a year or so. Up until now, she'd thought no one else had noticed. She sighed. *He made the soup himself...*

She reached over to the nightstand and pulled the card off the modest floral arrangement. *Might as well keep this away from prying eyes.* She slipped his sweet words of encouragement underneath her pillow. Such a nice man, but she'd never be able to commit herself to him—not with her heart believing that one day Lincoln might return.

"Almost ready. Just pouring some tea and getting a soup spoon..."

Celia's eyes fluttered shut as an almost-imperceptible smile formed on her lips.

Marcus picked up the pace as he headed home. He had lost all sense of time as he pruned, mulched and watered the church prayer garden. It had been so peaceful that his worries about Mama were all but forgotten for the entire afternoon. Frannie had brought Mama home last night. She'd been asleep when he left this morning, so he was looking forward to talking to her this afternoon.

Mandatory community service would end in a few weeks, but the Pastor had already asked him to consider a part-time paid position. Mrs. Samuelson and two of her neighbors also wanted Marcus to do their yard work twice a month. He'd be able to help Mama with the mounting medical bills and even—

Marcus stopped short as he rounded the corner. His chest tightened as he observed Mama's friend, dabbing at her eyes with a hankie as an ambulance pulled away from the house. "Mama." He ran toward Frannie. Mama was well, wasn't she? That was why she'd been released. Right?

He felt his heart in his throat, dizziness threatening to overtake him. Surely his mother hadn't... "No, no, no!" He took the steps two at a time.

Frannie grabbed onto his shoulders. Tears had already carved pathways down her rouged cheeks. "I'm so very sorry, Marcus. There was nothing they could do."

It was almost dusk when Marcus unclipped the leash from Baxter's collar and turned on the kitchen light. After filling the dog's dish with food, he walked down the hallway toward his mother's room. He rested his hand on the doorknob a moment before turning it and pushing the door open. He jumped when it creaked, laughing nervously. The pastor had told him there were no such things as ghosts. Still…

He flicked on the overhead light and walked around the bed, his hand trailing over its smooth wooden footboard, dresser, and finally the old treadle sewing machine. He picked up Mama's special music box and wound it. The colorful carousel came to life as three decorated horses pranced around its edge.

He smoothed her pillow and laid his head down on it, curling his knees up to his chest. He rocked back and forth, tears dampening the embroidered pillowcase. The air still smelled like Mama and he felt God's comforting presence. *Two hours. She's been gone only two hours.*

As he drifted off, he saw Mama's face—young and beautiful just as it was a decade ago as she bent down to tie his shoe.

"How was school today, my little man?"

"Okay, I guess."

He blinked his eyes as he awoke, observing the stillness of the carousel before he pulled the door shut and walked back down the hall toward the kitchen. His heartbeat quickened as the corner shelf that housed Mama's collection of teacups drew his attention. Before he could stop himself, he picked up Baxter's ball from the floor and threw it as hard as he could.

The teacups exploded one after another, as he aimed the ball repeatedly. When the shelf toppled to the floor, Marcus fell to his knees, heaving. *Mama, how could you leave me?*

He surveyed the damage. A broken mirror, cracked edge on the sink, an overturned pitcher of juice... Sifting through the broken dishes, he found that one matching cup and saucer were unharmed. He picked them up and placed them gently on the counter.

Tonight, their small yellow rosebuds looked oddly out of place.

Sitting in the first pew, two days later, Marcus stared at his mother's casket. He placed his finger inside his shirt collar and pulled at the neck. It was at least one size too small. Having barely been able to button it, he hid its stretched fabric underneath the sport coat he had borrowed from Frannie's husband.

He acknowledged Frannie's pat on his shoulder as she and Floyd took their seats behind him. "Isn't anyone else from the diner coming?" he whispered to her.

"Larry will be here, but everyone else had to work."

Pastor Brice climbed the two steps to the pulpit as Mrs. Filroy played the organ softly. Her dark hair cascaded down her shoulders and swished back and forth across her back in time with the music. "Like a River Glorious" was one of Mama's favorite songs. It sounded more beautiful now than ever.

The pastor looked at the clock and signaled for Mrs. Filroy to stop playing. "I will be reading today, from the Twenty-Third Psalm: *"The Lord is my Shepherd; I shall not want. He makes me to lie down in green pastures; He leads me beside the still waters. He restores my soul. He leads me in the paths of righteousness for His name's sake…"*

The pastor read on, but Marcus couldn't focus his attention on anything but the closed casket. He still pictured Mama as she had looked the night of the viewing. At first, he hadn't recognized her at all. Someone had curled her hair and fanned it out on the silken pillow, like the ladies in Hollywood movies. Not like Mama's at all. And Mama never wore makeup, but someone had put it on her face just the same. He shuddered. He would never be able to forget those red lips and rouged cheeks.

"Marcus. Marcus."

"Huh?"

"You'd like to say a few words, right?" Pastor Brice stepped aside, allowing space for him to stand behind the pulpit.

His legs were stiff as he settled himself behind the pulpit. He cleared his throat. Frannie, Floyd, Larry, the pastor, Simon's mother, and the organist were there. Not a crowd, but Marcus still felt his stomach flip-flop. He hoped he wouldn't throw up again, like he had last night when he saw Mama lying there...

The piece of notebook paper crinkled as he took it from his jacket pocket and unfolded it. "When my grandparents died, Mama read a verse from the Bible that said, 'To be absent from the body, is to be present with the Lord.' I know that's true. Mama's not in that box. She's with Jesus."

Marcus had known what he wanted to say—that Mama was the best mother any kid could ever hope to have...that she was kind and good and that she believed in him—but, as he looked at the faces staring back at him all he could think of was how he had disobeyed her...disappointed her...would never be able to live without her.

The room began to spin.

He vaguely heard someone say, "Breathe, Marcus, deep breaths—" before a blanket of darkness surrounded him.

Marcus replaced the second of two sympathy cards in its envelope and added it to the growing stack of junk mail and newspapers on the kitchen table. He ran his fingers through his uncombed hair. Walking to the cupboard, he removed one of four remaining cans of chicken noodle soup. He stared at the sink full of dirty dishes and shrugged. *No one will ever know...* He selected one of the pans, placed it on the coiled burner, and dumped in the contents of the can. *Maybe tomorrow night I'll eat with the Johnsons...*

A sharp knock at the door called Marcus away from the stove. He peeked out the curtain before turning the deadbolt.

When he opened the door, a woman in a powder blue suit shoved a business card into his hands. "I'm Marsha Steward. I'm a social worker. Are you Marcus Lickenberger?"

"Yes." Marcus's forehead furrowed as he squinted his eyes. He pushed his glasses upward with his forefinger.

The tall woman with a beehive hairdo barged into the room. She made her way down the hall and back, looking quickly into each room as she passed by. "Living here by yourself, are you?"

"Mama died last week."

"Looks to me like you could use a little help. I'll make some calls and find you some place to live temporarily. You're still a minor, you know. I've sent a certified letter to the man listed as your guardian. Didn't have a phone number, so we'll have to wait and see how he wants to handle the sale of the house and so on." Ms. Steward walked back into the kitchen, eyeing the sink, table, and broken dishes. "Looks like a teenage boy ought to be capable of cleaning up after himself, don't you think?"

Marcus hung his head. "I guess so."

"Good. Then what say you get busy on those dishes? After that, throw this mess in the garbage can, and take a shower. I'm sorry for your loss, Marcus. I understand being sad, son, I really do. However, you've got to get a grip and get on with your life."

"I already have a social worker. Mrs. Samuelson." Marcus looked at her with steady eyes, trying to stare her down like the cop on *Dragnet.*

"I'm aware of your past relationship due to community service, but your circumstances have changed. I'll be replacing her. Don't worry. Follow the rules and we'll get along fine, you and I."

"Yes, ma'am." Marcus traced the border of the floor tile with the toe of his slippers. *Busted...*

The social worker looked back over her shoulder as she went through the door. "By the way, no more skipping school. The principal is the one you can thank for this visit."

"Yes, ma'am."

After she left, Marcus headed back to the stove. Mrs. Samuelson was friendlier. He wasn't so sure this new lady was going to work out. As he stirred his dinner, he thought about who his guardian might be... and just how much homework he'd have this coming weekend.

Part Two

Then Peter came to Jesus and asked, "Lord, how many times shall I forgive my brother or sister who sins against me? Up to seven times?" Jesus answered, "I tell you, not seven times, but seventy-seven times."

Matthew 18: 21,22

Chapter Eight

"Raindrops Keep Fallin' On My Head" wafted from the boom box on the front porch as Marcus snipped painstakingly at the thorny branches of Mama's rose bush. Music made the job go faster and it also drowned out the menacing sounds coming from next door. *Was Simon in trouble again?* Marcus had three yards to do today, so he couldn't be spending time worrying about what went on over there. *Still...*

He looked up as an older Cadillac Coupe de Ville pulled into the driveway. A lanky guy in jeans and a faded T-shirt pulled his long legs out of the car and stretched before shutting the door. He stood on the driveway, staring at Marcus before walking over to him. "This Celia Lickenberger's house?"

"Mama died last week." Marcus blocked out the sun with his bent arm, trying to get a good look at the visitor.

"And I suppose you're Marcus, are 'ya?" The man removed his cowboy hat, smoothed his thin hair back with his free hand, and then returned the hat to his head.

"Yes, sir."

"Well, my name is Lincoln. I'm your—your—"

Marcus felt his heart double-thump. His head spun. "Father?"

"Sit down, boy, before you fall down."

Marcus lowered himself to sit on the lawnmower. He took several deep breaths. *What's he doing here?*

"How about we go down to McDonald's, get us some lunch and visit a bit?"

"I—I—I'm busy."

"I can see that." Lincoln surveyed the yard. "Your Mama always did love roses, didn't she?"

"What would *you* know about it?"

Lincoln cleared his throat. "Let's not get off on the wrong foot, Marcus. The yard work will still be here when you get back, don't you suppose?"

Marcus studied Lincoln's face—bushy mustache, wisps of dark brown hair sticking out from underneath his hat. Funny. He'd never pictured his father as being a cowboy. He shrugged his shoulders. "I guess so." He let the hedge clippers drop to the ground, his legs wobbling as he stood. He could feel the hair on his head standing on end. He took a deep breath. He'd wanted nothing more his whole life than to meet his father, so why was he suddenly so afraid?

A few minutes later, they sat in a small booth at a nearby McDonald's, both staring at the table between them.

Marcus drummed his fingers on the Formica top. He never saw this day coming. As the years passed, having a father had become a distant reality. Relieved when their order's number was finally called, Marcus jumped up from his seat. "I'll get it."

He retrieved the tray, unloading drinks, fries, and burgers onto the table. It wasn't until he took his last bite that he looked into the eyes of the man he had dreamed of meeting for the last seventeen years. Now, however, he wondered just why.

"So, are you making it okay, now that—well, you know." Lincoln stuffed his last French fry into his mouth.

"Okay, I guess."

"How old are you now?"

"You don't know?"

"I guess I lost track over the years."

Marcus gave him a hard look. He'd often thought of his father as someone who'd wondered, from time to time, just how he and his mother were—someone who'd driven by the house on sleepless nights hoping for a glimpse of his son—and the wife he'd once loved. Now he knew the truth. Marcus stood up, not quite knowing what to do next. "Thanks for lunch. I've got to go."

"Whoa. Sit back down. We've got some things to sort out. Some decisions have to be made."

Still standing, Marcus asked, "Like what?"

"Please sit, Marcus." Lincoln motioned for Marcus to reclaim his place at the table.

He hadn't ever so much as laid his eyes on Marcus and now his father was going to make decisions? His face grew hot as he slid back into the seat across from Lincoln. "What kind of decisions?"

"For starters, where you're going to live—and with whom." Lincoln took a small notepad, reading glasses, and ballpoint pen out of his coat pocket. As he clicked the pen, he added, "Do you have any feelings about it one way or another?"

Marcus gulped. His heart was beating in his throat. "Do I have a choice?"

Lincoln pushed the glasses that had slid down his nose back up with his thumb. "Well, as I understand it, you can go into a foster home until you're eighteen. After that, you may qualify to live in a group home. Then, I guess it's remotely possible that you'd be able to live on your own in an apartment. I'm not real sure about that one."

"Can't I keep staying at home, like I have been?"

"I need to meet with the state's attorney, but I'm under the impression that it was your mother's wishes that the house be put up for sale and the money used to pay for your living expenses. The house won't bring that much, it being so small and in an older area of the city. It looks like it's paid for, though. She must have been quite a saver to get that much money put away. She was frugal and made every penny count. That's for sure."

"You haven't talked with her—or even seen her—since I was born. How do you know what she wants?"

"I've been appointed to be your guardian, Marcus. The court sent me a letter and I met with your mother's attorney, yesterday. I need to move things along quickly, so I can get back home to my job and m—my—"

"Your what?"

"My, um, family." He sucked air in between his teeth. "Sorry."

Marcus slammed his fist onto the table. "I can't believe this. You're my guardian. *You* get to make decisions about *me,* and you have a family? Kids?"

Lincoln cleared his throat and then unbuttoned his collar. "I—I'm married to a very nice lady, Marcus, and yes, we have two boys."

Marcus's head swam. *A wife? Boys?*

"I know this is a lot to take in. It is for me, too. I mean, I never thought I'd be meeting you. And I sure never knew I'd be expected to make any decisions concerning you. For all I knew you were—"

"Yeah. Well, I understand more than you think I do. I know you didn't want me, or you would have never left. I know you didn't love Mama. She was wonderful. She did her job. Yours, too. She never said one bad word about you, but I heard your name at least once every day. You know why? She prayed for you at supper *every single night.* You might have forgotten *us*, but she never forgot *you.*" He grabbed a napkin and swiped at the tears that found their way down his cheeks and onto his grass-stained T-shirt.

"Marcus, there's no way I'm ever going to get you to understand how things were."

"Well, don't worry about me. I'll just stay at home until you kick me out. How's that? Then I'll go to one of those group homes. Live with other guys like me that don't have families—" He glared at Lincoln's chalk-white face. He started for the door; then stopped and turned back.

"I'm seventeen."

He'd walked toward home in a fog, completely unaware of people or traffic. His thoughts were a jumbled mess. Why had Mama thought anything good could ever come out of Lincoln being made his guardian? He would have done just fine on his own. He certainly didn't need a man that had a wife and two sons to tell him what to do.

He was just rounding the corner to Ash Avenue when he heard someone call his name. "Is that you, Marcus?"

He used his hand to shield his eyes from the sun. "Sally?"

"Yeah. It's me." Her face was blotchy, mascara smudged underneath her eyes.

"Are you okay?"

"Not really."

"What are you doing here?"

She stared at Marcus for a moment before she continued. "I'm waiting for Simon." She motioned for him to follow her to a nearby bench. She sat down, patting a place beside her. "Can you sit awhile?"

"Me?"

She blotted her eyes and blew her nose. "Just for a few minutes?"

"Okay. Sure." He slid onto the far end of the bench. "Why are you crying?"

"I'm in b—big trouble, M—Marcus." Sally fished a tissue out of her sweater pocket.

"What do you mean?"

She cocked her head. "You won't tell anybody, will you?"

Marcus shook his head.

Sally let out a long breath. “I’m pregnant.”

“Whoa. You mean you’re going to have a b—baby?”

She nodded, crying between hiccups.

He winced. “Does it hurt?”

“No, Marcus. I’m not having the baby *now*.”

“Oh, then—”

“I’m crying because I’m upset. I don’t want to have a baby…and I don’t want to tell Simon. But I have to.”

“Is it *his* baby?”

Sally nodded. “He’s going to be mad. Then his parents are going to be upset. His dad has such a temper, you know. He’ll beat him for sure. I’m worried about the baby and what to do and Simon and his parents, and—” She clamped her hand onto his and held on. “My own parents kicked me out.”

His hand lost all feeling as she kept squeezing. He could only think of his own mother and how she had struggled over the years to take care of him. What would happen to Sally and the baby? Would Simon leave them in the same way Lincoln had left him and Mama?

That evening, Marcus was watching television when Simon knocked on the door.

“Wanna go for a ride?”

Marcus raised his eyebrows. “Me? With you?”

“Come on.” He snatched Marcus’s flannel shirt off the hook, shoved it into his arms, and pushed him out the open doorway.

"Where'd you get that shiner?" Marcus blurted out. He'd meant to be careful not to mention any of the marks or bruises he'd seen, lately, especially since Simon had gone ballistic when he had done so several months ago. Why had he done it now? Was it because the baby was on his mind?

"None of your business."

Marcus hesitated before going down the steps two at a time and hopping into the front seat of Simon's car. "Wh—where are we going?"

"I thought we'd just cruise around for a while. Maybe drink a few of these." Simon reached over the back seat, producing a six-pack of beer. He gave one to Marcus and then popped the top off another. He took a quick drink, forced a smile, and then pulled away from the curb. "Don't be a sissy."

Marcus took a long look at the can.

"You're a man now, Marcus. You're on your own. No rules. You're gonna love it. Trust me."

He'd felt dizzy after the first sip. His stomach was upset after the second. But somehow it felt good to Marcus, being a man and all.

Two beers and twenty minutes later, Simon drove past the Arizona Ambulance Company, circled around, and parked two streets over, next to an abandoned building. "Hop out. We're gonna say hello to a guy who works here." He grabbed a beer and started down the sidewalk.

An old guy with '*CARL*' embroidered on his shirt met them at the gate. "What are you young fellas up to?"

"Just thought we'd bring you a beer—and this." As soon as Carl reached out for the beer, Simon grabbed him and wrestled him to the ground. He pulled out a roll of duct tape from his jacket pocket and taped the guy's hands behind his back. Then he put a large piece of it over his mouth. "Thanks, Carl." He placed the beer about a foot away from his hands. "In case you get thirsty before morning." He stared at the old guy, his lip curling at the corner.

"Marcus, get the key. We're going for a joy ride, you and me." Simon stumbled toward the only ambulance in the lot—red and white with '*AAC*' stenciled on the door.

Marcus plucked the key from the pegboard and followed. "I don't feel so good, Simon. Let's go home." It was wrong to steal. But in spite of what the pastor had said Marcus still felt compelled to follow Simon's orders.

Simon snatched the key from Marcus's hand. "Not a chance, buddy. Hop in. If you feel like puking, let me know and I'll pull over."

Simon started the motor and backed the long ambulance out of the parking spot. "Better shut your door, or you'll fall out," he joked.

Marcus had no sooner closed it than he started to feel sick again. When he saw an open field on his side of the road, he yelled for Simon to pull over.

When Simon slowed down, Marcus flung the door open and fell onto the hard ground. He retched for several minutes before crawling back toward Simon, who'd left the vehicle and was now sitting in the dirt, propped against the ambulance door.

Simon took another swig of his beer and popped a handful of Cheetos into his mouth before shoving the bag at Marcus. "Here, you need to get something on your stomach. I should've known you couldn't handle it."

Marcus shoveled in half of the bag before rolling onto his back. "Let's go home, Simon."

"How do you know if you love someone, Marcus?" Simon leaned his head back, looking up at the dark night sky.

"What are you talking about?"

"I'm talking about Sally, of course." Simon paused, biting his lip before continuing. "I mean, she's pretty and sweet and smart. What's not to love, right?"

"I guess so." Marcus had noticed those same qualities in Sally more than once, himself, but confessing that to Simon would only get him into trouble.

Simon swiped at the tears beginning to trickle down his cheeks. "But I'm just not ready for—for—what I mean is I want to get away from here…see the world…have some adventures. I don't even know what love is. That's why I asked you—because your mom loved you. So, what *is* love, anyway?"

Marcus's thoughts went back to Mama, shaking the last of her tip money out of the jar so he could get an ice cream cone. "I guess it's when you care about someone more than yourself."

Simon thought for a minute and then shook his head. "Nah. That can't be it. I should've known better than to ask a kid like you."

Marcus shrugged. Yeah, what would he know? But he sure knew what love *wasn't.* It wasn't a father who beat you, like Simon's did. And it sure wasn't a cowboy who left his son in the hospital and then showed up seventeen years later and bought him a burger and fries.

The warmth of the sun on his face woke Marcus with a start. He looked at his surroundings. It seemed they were in a cotton field. Fluffy white balls dotted the landscape in every direction. He rubbed his hands over his belly, wincing at its fullness. Too many Cheetos. Too much beer.

It was already morning…the first time he'd ever slept a night away from home. He smiled, not sure what part of last night's experience made him happy. Maybe it was just the fact that he'd made it through the night. "Hey, wake up." His loud belch woke Simon with a start.

Simon grabbed the door handle and pulled himself up. He took the last swallow from the Coors can and tossed it over his shoulder. "I must've fallen asleep." He rubbed his eyes and then yawned as he surveyed the candy wrappers and potato chips littering the ground. "Wow. Did we do all this?"

Marcus nodded. "We're in big trouble. We'd better get the ambulance back."

"Nah. And miss the best part? Not on your life." Simon swung the ambulance door open, hopped in, and turned the key in the ignition. "Get in and switch on the siren."

Marcus grinned as he settled himself into the seat next to Simon, his sometimes-friend and always arch-enemy. He hovered his trembling fingers over the large red button. "The flashers on, too, Simon?"

"Sure. Got to warn people to get out of our way, don't we? The Marauders are comin' on through. Oh, yeah." Simon's eyes lit with a devious spark.

"Who are the Marauders?"

"Us, you twerp."

Simon pulled onto the highway, a heavy fog of dust billowing up behind them. "Look out, world. Here we come."

Marcus's heartbeat increased to match the accelerating speed of the ambulance as it sped down dusty trails on the outskirts of Phoenix. Even after reaching the city limits, Simon didn't slow the vehicle down. It barreled through intersection after intersection. "You're going to get us killed."

Ignoring a series of barricades—and the warning from Marcus—Simon swerved around heavy road equipment being used for road construction. "Whew. What a rush." He turned toward Marcus with a huge grin on his face.

"Stop! A hole!" Marcus splayed his hands against the dash and pushed the soles of his feet against the floorboard. This was a roller-coaster ride he'd never forget. "Do something."

Simon's hair stood on end, eyes bulging. "It's the hole or crash into the grader."

"Grader."

Simon turned the wheel sharply to the left. Moments later, the ambulance hit the grader at top speed, flipping high into the air before it landed with a loud thud, rolled over and came to rest on the edge of darkness.

Chapter Nine

Hanging upside down by his seatbelt at the base of South Mountain, Marcus came to just as huge hands yanked Simon out of the vehicle.

Simon squirmed to free himself. "Hey, get your hands off me."

"Now, hold on. Let's see if you've got any injuries and take it from there. All right?"

"I'm fine. Just let go of me."

"Not so quick, young man. Mind telling me just what you boys thought you were doing? Stealing an emergency vehicle is a felony, you know." The handle of the gun in the holster glistened in the light of the blinking emergency lights. "So is drinking and driving."

"I don't know what got into him, officer. He said he had a gun in his pocket and ordered me to drive this stolen vehicle. I was just trying to keep from getting myself killed." Simon leaned for a moment against the upside-down hood of the smoking ambulance and then jumped back at the heat rising from the engine. He waved a blistered hand back and forth, blowing on it.

Marcus winced at the pain in his shoulder and then shook his head to clear it. *A gun?* He'd never even seen one up close. As he was cut loose from the seatbelt, Marcus dropped to the ground, scrambling over dry brush to the safety of a nearby boulder. He shook his head. When would he ever learn he couldn't trust Simon? Why had he even gone with him in the first place?

The burly officer walked over to him, pulling off his glasses and massaging the bridge of his nose before replacing them. "What about it, son? Did you pull a weapon on this young man?" He bent down, coming nose to nose with Marcus. "Have you been drinking, too?"

Marcus's eyes teared up. He wiped his runny nose with the sleeve of his shirt. He knew better than to snitch on Simon, fearing any of a number of reprisals. Still, he should tell the truth to the law...He stole a look in Simon's direction, nodding his head ever so slightly.

A thin line of blood trickled from a cut on Simon's lower lip. He licked it away, glaring at Marcus. "You might as well come clean. You know what happens when you try to pin your misdeeds on someone else, don't you? Yeah, *you* know."

Truth was, Marcus did know. Simon would be glad to lay the blame on him because Marcus was too weak to stand up for himself and tell the truth. Simon was a smooth talker. A "contemptible liar" was what Mama had once called him.

Simon gritted his teeth and leaned close. "Don't be a snitch," he whispered into Marcus's ear before turning toward the officer. "Don't be too hard on him, though, Officer, he just found out he's gonna be a daddy." He slapped his hand on Marcus's back.

Had he heard Simon correctly? Why would he tell such a lie?

The officer shifted his gaze from Marcus to Simon and back again. He shook his head as he looked down at the urine pooling onto the hard earth between Marcus's outstretched legs.

February was one of the longest months of his life. Marcus had a hard time adjusting to the occasional visits from Lincoln, as well as spending nights in Frannie's spare bedroom. The rule had been imposed by his father—in exchange for his freedom after school to do his chores at home, including the feeding and walking of Baxter. He found that if he hurried, he was left with enough time to eat, shower, and watch a little television before walking over to the Johnsons' large two-story house, only three blocks away.

For the most part, Lincoln had kept his distance, only checking up on Marcus by occasionally phoning Frannie. Only now and then, he actually made an appearance, usually when he was showing the house to prospective buyers.

But today was different. It was the sentencing, following last week's hearing. Marcus tried to pull away as Lincoln half-dragged him up the concrete steps to the courthouse entrance. He hung his head. In his overwhelming desire for friendship and belonging, he had allowed Simon to have free rein over his actions. No, if he was completely honest, he'd gone with Simon to show Lincoln that he was a tough guy…that he could handle things by himself…he could do what he wanted…he didn't need *him.*

His guardian ran his finger down the list posted outside the chamber door. "M. Lickenberger—4:30 P.M."

They slipped into the courtroom, taking seats in the back row. While they waited, Marcus observed the sentencing of a guy for driving under the influence. He glanced over at Lincoln, his head back against the wall and his hat pulled down over his eyes. He was probably thinking about Betty's visit last night. She'd come by to let Marcus know that the adult court judge had sentenced Simon, now eighteen, to three years in prison. There had been a man working down in that hole. When the ambulance jarred the ground, falling dirt had cut off his air supply. The rescue crew arrived too late to save him. The thought that they were murderers weighed heavy on Marcus's heart.

Marcus liked Betty. After all, she'd been the only woman in the neighborhood willing to babysit Marcus when Mama needed to go to an appointment or work overtime. Betty had never treated him like he was different. She always had a warm cookie and a glass of cold milk waiting for him.

Mama had told Marcus that they had to bear up under Simon's poor behavior for the sake of keeping the peace between the families. But he knew, even at that young age, what she'd meant was that they needed to stay in the good graces of his babysitter.

Last night, Lincoln told Betty that Mama had used poor judgment in letting Marcus be around Simon. He said Betty's own reluctance to stand up to her husband had contributed to Simon's delinquency—and the truancy of his own son.

"Marcus Lickenberger."

Tensing when the bailiff called his name, Marcus latched onto Lincoln's arm as they both stood. His legs reluctantly carried him forward.

"Here." Lincoln nudged him with his elbow and then thrust a glass of water into his hand.

Marcus gulped it down, saying a silent prayer that something would happen to somehow cancel the proceedings. A wildfire might be a little too dangerous. A tornado, perhaps?

Lincoln gave him a slight push forward and returned to his own seat in the back row.

Somehow Marcus managed to meet his state-appointed attorney in front of the bench, facing the judge. He pulled on a loose thread, causing a shirt button to drop to the floor. He chased it as it rolled to the other side of the room. Finally, it wobbled and came to rest beneath the prosecuting attorney's table. Marcus crawled underneath to retrieve it, stuck it in his pocket and then tucked his gaping shirt back into the waistband of his new pants.

The Honorable J.J. Jenkins cleared his throat. "Let's get back to the business at hand, shall we?" As the laughter in the courtroom died down, he turned to Marcus. "Son, I have given careful consideration to your case in light of your disabilities. It seems that your association with an older boy has influenced your behavior throughout your childhood, and now into your teenage years. My advice to you is to disengage yourself from him, think about what your actions have done to your family, and form a new set of habits that will ensure a happy and productive life ahead for you as an adult. Seven months' probation." The gavel came down hard.

"Mama! Mama! I'm sorry, Mama!" Marcus's voice was lost in the chaos that erupted in the room.

"Next case, Thomas Morris."

Marcus lifted the calendar from Carson's Mortuary off the nail near the door. Turning the first page, he found March and then counted off the next seven months. Starting today, at the sentencing, probation would be over before the end of the year. He grabbed the red marker from the junk drawer and circled *October 31* next to a picture of Snoopy and the gang trick-or-treating.

Due to the lateness of the sentencing, Lincoln had called Frannie and told her he'd be spending the night at the house with Marcus and driving back to Tucson the next morning. By the time they had eaten an order of fish and chips and driven home, it was eight o'clock. Lincoln dragged himself to Mama's bed, saying he'd just let himself out about six a.m. and get on the road, it being a two-hour drive to Tucson.

Yawning, Marcus turned out the light and walked across the hall to his bedroom. He sat down on the three-legged stool by the bed, removed his new shoes, then his socks. He winced as he touched the flap of skin hanging from his heel. He'd told Lincoln he didn't need new shoes for court, but his father had said he wouldn't have him looking like an orphan in front of a judge. *Well, wasn't that just dandy?* He packed the shoes back into the box they'd come in and shoved them to the back of the closet.

He bent down the window blind with his pinky, looking at the now-deserted corner where the guys used to play baseball. He sighed, wishing he could turn back the clock to see one of their games just one more time.

Letting the blind go, he stooped over to pet Baxter, already asleep beside the bed. He thought of Lincoln and his wife and boys. One big happy family. A life so different from his own…

Marcus folded his shirt and placed it on top of his Dockers. When he sank into the softness of the bed, his thoughts turned to Mama. He flopped onto his side, scrunched up his pillow and looked toward the darkened kitchen door. He imagined Mama, sitting at the table reading her Bible before bedtime and then pausing at his door to say goodnight after she'd finished her prayers. *Oh, Mama, I miss you.*

He wiped his tears on the pillow. He felt guilty for crying. After all, here he was in a nice warm bed, while Simon slept on a hard bunk next to a toilet and had food slid to him under the cell door. He thought back over the past couple of months—stealing the ambulance, the poor man in the hole, Sally and Simon's baby…

An hour later, Marcus woke with a start, his heart hammering in his chest. He sat up and swung his legs over the side of the bed. As he ran his fingers through his damp hair, his thoughts cleared. Another nightmare. Couldn't he at least be freed from Simon in his dreams?

He peeled off his pajama bottoms and placed them in the washer along with the wet sheets. Then he curled up on the braided rug next to Baxter and rocked himself to sleep.

The following Saturday morning, Marcus ran his tongue around the edges of the bowl of oatmeal. Betty sure was a good cook. Left over from her own breakfast this morning, she had told Marcus she was having trouble learning to make less, now that Simon wasn't living at home. Her eyes had been bloodshot when she'd knocked on his door with the steaming bowl of cooked cereal. She was already missing her son. Marcus would, too, in a strange sort of way.

Pastor Brice's smiling face appeared in the window of the kitchen door. "Can I come in?" When Marcus motioned him inside, he pushed the door open and made himself at home.

"Betty made oatmeal." Marcus winced as the pastor lowered himself into Mama's chair. "There's plenty, if you're hungry."

"Thanks, Marcus, but I've already eaten." He folded his hands on the table. "Well, son, the judge somehow sorted out everything just right. From now on, stay close to home when you're not working. By the time Simon gets out, maybe you'll have forgotten all about him."

"Simon lied about the baby, you know. It's his, not mine."

"I guessed as much."

"In your sermon, you said people have to forgive each other. But Pastor Brice, I don't understand why. I mean, people do wrong things to us and then we're supposed to just tell them it's okay?"

"No. You can tell them that what they do hurts you and even that it's not all right. But forgiveness means that you choose not to hold it against them. Forgiveness is about the *past,* but it's for the *future*—and it's for *the offended* just as much, if not more, than *the offender.*"

"I don't understand."

"Forgiveness makes it possible for you to have a relationship on down the road."

"Oh, no. I'm never going to be friends with Simon."

"Maybe not. However, somewhere along the line one of you might need some help or something. It's a lot easier to be there for someone if you no longer harbor bad feelings about them."

"I don't think I'll ever be able to forget all the things he's done to me."

"No, but the memory of them will fade over time. When you let it go, you can find freedom from the past."

"He lied about the drugs. Then he lied about the ambulance. He even said the baby was *mine.* How many times do I have to forgive him?"

"The Bible says seventy times seven."

Marcus jumped to his feet, his heart pounding. "I guess I'm just a no-good person, then, because there is no way I could ever do that."

"It will surprise you, no doubt, but you'll be able to, in time. And I know you don't want to hear this, but there's someone else that's in need of forgiveness, too."

He knew the pastor meant Lincoln. "I don't want to talk about him."

"It may take a while, but someday you'll understand just why forgiving is so important."

Sally came to the doorway and stopped. After a yawn and a long overhead stretch, she leaned against the facing and stared at the pastor.

"And who might you be?" Pastor Brice stood, offering her his chair.

"I'm Sally. I'm staying here for a little while."

Marcus winced. *Why in the world did she say that? I'll likely get in trouble for not showing up at Frannie's last night. Please, Sally, don't make it worse than it is…*

The pastor rubbed his chin. "Simon's girlfriend?"

"Yes. I mean, no. Well, sort of." She brushed the hair away from her face.

His eyes widened. "The girl who's having Simon's baby?"

"Marcus, you weren't supposed to say anything—you know, until everything is decided," she whispered.

Marcus shook his head, took his bowl to the sink and added more soap to the cold dishwater. When he ran more hot water from the faucet, bubbles rose to the surface—and burst.

After the pastor left, Sally called to Marcus from the open hall closet. "Let's play a game of Dominos." She pulled the game off the shelf, pushed the door closed with her elbow, and joined Marcus at the kitchen table. "You'll have to move all those coupons."

Just a few minutes ago, she was scolding me for telling the pastor she was going to have a baby. Now she wants to play a game? Marcus finished cutting out a coupon for Cheerios before he looked up. "This is a good way to save money."

"Mom uses them, too. I just meant that you need to move them, so we can play." Sally shooed him with a flick of her wrist.

"I don't want to play Dominos. I want to know why you told the pastor that you were staying here. It was only for one night, Sally, that's what you said, 'one night,' right?"

"Well, it could be a *little* longer if I can't find another place. You wouldn't want a pregnant mother to sleep on the sidewalk, would you?" She rolled her eyes and placed a hand on her hip.

His shoulders slumped. "No, but you can't stay here. Lincoln has the house for sale and people will come to look at it. He says it can't be messy. I even have to make my bed every day. Anyway, only married people can live in the same house."

"Oh, Marcus. That's not true. Two of my aunts live together. They're not married. Our teacher's father lives with her. They're not married." Sally laughed and pushed his arm playfully.

Marcus scowled at her. "You know what I mean."

"I guess." Sally shrugged her shoulders and started removing Dominos from the box.

"I said I don't want to play." Marcus shoved the cut coupons into an envelope and tacked it onto the small bulletin board next to the window. "I'm taking Baxter for his walk."

"Come on, Marcus. Just for a few minutes?" She clasped her hands together in front of her, begging like a puppy.

"Listen, I—" Marcus heard giggling outside a second before the doorbell chimed. He started for the door, but Sally pushed past him. She flung the door open. "Sherry. Laura. What a surprise. Come on in," she gushed.

Two girls Marcus recognized from school rushed into the living room, hugging Sally as they entered. Both girls sat down on the couch, kicked off their shoes and tucked their bare feet underneath them.

"Make yourselves at home, why don't you?"

Laura turned toward Marcus. "Have any soda?"

Chapter Ten

Waiting in line to leave the sanctuary, Marcus thanked God that Sally had agreed to attend church with him this morning. He knew she hadn't gone with her parents since she'd told them about the baby, three months ago. Her father had called her a sinner "of the worst kind" and her pastor said she couldn't worship at their church any longer.

Marcus hoped that getting her reconnected with God would keep her from choosing an abortion, like Simon suggested, or going back east to live with her aunt until the baby's birth and then giving it up for adoption, as her mother hoped she would.

Sally hadn't wanted anyone else to know that she was pregnant, in case she decided to get the abortion, but he'd spoiled that by telling the pastor. It was better that he'd told him, anyway. *Maybe Pastor Brice will be able to convince her to keep the baby.*

He followed Sally to the gleaming mahogany doors where Pastor Brice stood shaking hands with the mother of a small baby in a buggy. When the pastor reached into his pocket and produced a lollipop for the child's older sister, the girl took off down the steps with a giggle and a wave.

"Well, Sally, it's a pleasure to have you worship with us today." Pastor Brice placed a hand on her shoulder. "I'm glad Marcus invited you. I should have done that myself, yesterday when we met."

"Thank you for welcoming me, even though I know I don't deserve to be here." She hung her head, focusing on a clump of grass growing between the stepping stones.

"That's where you're wrong, young lady. This is most definitely where you belong." Pastor Brice reached inside to flick off the sanctuary lights and then produced a key and locked the doors. "Everyone's welcome in God's house. Don't you forget that."

Marcus could hear her loud gulp and couldn't help but notice that her face had turned red. Before he realized it, he'd grabbed her hand and given it a quick squeeze.

Sally slowly lifted her eyes to meet the pastor's. "What I mean is, I'm a sinner," her voice barely above a whisper.

"We *all* are, my dear. If we weren't, we wouldn't need God. Now, would we?"

"I—I." Sally's lip trembled. She grabbed Marcus's elbow to steady her.

"Some people feel they have to be good enough—you know—*worthy* to come to church, but in fact, God accepts us as we *are*."

"Pregnant? Not married? Does he accept someone like that? Like *me?*"

"He does, indeed. Tell you what, why don't you come by the church office sometime on Thursday and we'll have ourselves a nice, long chat. Maybe I'll be able to convince you that there's nothing you have done that God isn't willing to forgive. Will you do that?"

Sally nodded and then quickly hugged Pastor Brice. "Thank you."

He held her for a few minutes as she cried it out. When he stepped back, he placed his straw hat onto his head and started down the shady sidewalk toward the prayer garden.

After eating at Bill's Burgers, Marcus and Sally entered the house, laughing at a joke she had told for the second time. Marcus didn't mind. In fact, he was glad she had retold it because he was trying to memorize it to use on the pastor the next time he saw him. It was about a priest, so Marcus was sure he'd find the humor in it. Problem was, each time Marcus tried to retell it, he messed up the punch line.

Marcus stopped short when he saw Lincoln, sitting in a kitchen chair, his legs out in front of him, crossed at the ankles.

"You're finally home, I see." Lincoln's sarcasm ruined an otherwise pleasant afternoon.

Marcus felt a sinking feeling in the pit of his stomach. "Wh—what are you doing here?"

"I'm showing the house at two-thirty. Drove up from Tucson after breakfast. I was hopin' to find the house in better condition than this—dishes and garbage piled up, bed unmade. I'm sure I cautioned you 'bout how I expect you to keep the house lookin' nice while it's for sale."

Marcus sighed. "Yes, sir."

Lincoln sucked air in between his teeth—an irritating habit of his. "And just who might this be, hidin' behind your back?"

Sally walked around Marcus, glaring in a way that told Marcus she already didn't like his father. "I'm Sally. A friend of your son's."

Lincoln shook his head, turning to sneer at Marcus. "This girl is likely to get you in trouble, Marcus. She barely looks sixteen." Lincoln stared back at her with equal distaste.

Sally straightened, lifting her chin. "I'll have you know I'll be seventeen this coming Friday."

"Just as I thought. Eighteen is the legal age in this state f—for—oh, never mind. Anyway, I don't expect the Watkins for another twenty minutes, so get busy and make this place presentable."

Marcus hustled off to his room. He yanked the sheet and bedspread up over the pillow, gathered dirty clothes from the floor and tossed them into the laundry hamper.

Sally remained riveted to the spot in front of Lincoln, wearing that defiant grin that Marcus had seen so much of in the past few weeks. "Who are you to make yourself at home, here, and bark orders at Marcus?"

Marcus slid across the hallway and pulled on Sally's arm. "Come help me with the dishes."

Sally smirked. "In a minute. I want to hear what this guy has to say for himself, first."

Lincoln cleared his throat. "I am, young lady, Marcus's f—fa—I mean, guardian."

Sally placed her hands on her hips. "Ah, so you can't even say the word 'father' without choking on it, can you? I suppose that's because you have no idea what it means to be one. Isn't that right?"

"I may have not been there for Marcus, but what kind of a father is it that kicks his pregnant daughter out of the house?" Lincoln spat the words out from beneath his mustache.

Sally stared at Marcus for a moment, her mouth hanging open. "Marcus, is there anyone you haven't told?" She turned and fled down the steps. Along the sidewalk she scuttled, her shoulders heaving. Marcus could still hear her wailing long after she turned the corner and disappeared from sight.

He grabbed a bag of garbage and flung the back door open, heading for the alley. "What did you have to do that for? Life's hard enough for her right now without you adding to it," he yelled over his shoulder.

He hung out in the backyard while the prospective buyers looked at the house. A few minutes later, he heard Lincoln's car start up. By the time he came back in, Lincoln had already driven away. *He didn't even say good-bye.*

A few hours later, Lincoln called to tell him that the couple hadn't wanted the house. "Be sure to keep it looking tip-top from now on. We need to get it sold, Marcus."

Replacing the phone in the cradle, Marcus headed for the kitchen, turning on lights as he went. *Why is*

Lincoln blaming me? I can't help it that the couple didn't like the house. Maybe they want three bedrooms...or maybe they don't like this neighborhood. And the fact that Lincoln was still ranting about Sally's disrespect didn't bother him one bit, either. Fact of the matter was, Marcus kind of liked the way she had stood up to his father.

Except for Mama and Pastor Brice, he couldn't remember anyone else ever caring enough to defend him before. It felt good—even if Sally was Simon's girl.

The week went by quickly, except for the times when Marcus thought about Sally. He wondered where she'd run off to after the head-to-head with Lincoln. Had she perhaps gone to a girlfriend's house? Or, maybe her parents had changed their minds and asked her to come back home? At any rate, she'd finally phoned early this morning, saying she'd drop by after supper. He'd be sure to get his questions answered then.

Marcus fed Baxter, took him for a walk around the block, and watched the Spider-Man movie before he took a shower. Now, with his hair combed and a clean T-shirt on, he took the pink-frosted cupcake out of the small cardboard box and placed it on the table. He opened the junk drawer, rummaging around for a candle. He found a pink one that had only been burned part of the way down and stuck it into the gooey icing.

He licked the two fingers that had touched the frosting. *Yum.* He looked forward to seeing the surprised look on Sally's face. He lowered himself into his chair at the table and kept his eyes on the door until they grew too heavy to keep open.

He massaged the kink out of his neck. Had he fallen asleep? Was it Saturday morning? He peered out the kitchen window. It was already light outside. He slipped a couple of pieces of bread into the toaster. What had happened to Sally? Had she forgotten her promise?

He could feel his anger welling at her rudeness. He finished his toast and apple juice and then headed outside. He was in a foul mood. He gave the lawnmower a kick when it failed to start up on the first pull. *Oh, Sally, what are you doing to me?*

Later, he rode his bike to the neighborhood grocery store. Saturday was his favorite day to shop because Mr. Germann, the store's owner, gave out free samples. As he looked for the shortest sample line, he spotted Sally at the checkout counter. "Hey, Sally. Wait up."

She froze for a moment. Then she grabbed her bag and headed for the door.

Marcus followed, weaving in and out of the crowded store and finally into the parking lot. "Hey, didn't you hear me?"

Sally called back over her shoulder, "Yes. I did, but just go away, Marcus. Leave me alone."

What? Did I hear her right? "You're in a hurry?"

"To get away from you."

"But—but, I don't understand. Did I do—?"

"Just keep away from me, that's all."

Marcus stood amid the parked cars, watching Sally disappear down the street. He felt like he had been punched in the stomach. Why was she acting so strange? What could he have possibly done to make her turn against him this way?

Monday morning, Marcus headed in the direction of his locker. He still felt no better about things between him and Sally. He had talked to Frannie about it Saturday night, but she couldn't come up with any answers either. All he could do was hope she had gotten over whatever it was and was back to her normal self. If not, it was going to be a long, miserable summer without her to talk to.

All of a sudden, someone bumped him hard from behind, smashing his face up against the metal door with a bang. "Oops, sorry."

Marcus brought his hand up just in time to catch the first drops of blood. He eyed the sleeve of his shirt, but instead pulled a piece of lined paper out of his spiral notebook and held it up to his nose. "Did you do that on purpose?"

"What? Me? No. No. It was totally an accident," the tall, curly-headed guy replied with a smirk.

He's one of Simon's friends. He was in the car when Colin gave me the bag…

"Hey, what's going on here? Break it up, ladies and gentlemen, and get on to your classes." Principal Herrington's huge frame loomed just a few feet in front of Marcus. "Get yourself down to the Nurse's office, son. You're making a mess of my hallway."

Snickers erupted from the large crowd that had formed around the boys. Marcus was shocked to see Sally was among them and had joined in the laughter.

He slammed his locker door shut, slipped between several onlookers and headed down the hallway. *So that's how it is. What a fool I've been. When she needs a favor or a place to stay, it's "Oh, Marcus, please. You're such a nice guy." But at school, she's embarrassed to be seen with me.*

It had been a long week, but Thursday afternoon finally had come. He'd thought about ditching the last couple of days of school. Grades were in, so it really wouldn't have mattered. However, Frannie always drove him to school on her way to work, so there was no way of getting out of it. Anyway, it was over now, and the long summer stretched ahead. At least he wouldn't have to be ignored by Sally every day in third period.

Next year they'd be seniors. Could he endure this for another year?

He lifted the lid on the metal mailbox and reached inside. He pulled out a rather thick envelope with Arizona State Prison System stamped in the upper left-hand corner. *Probably something about my probation...* He slipped his key in the lock and braced himself for Baxter's greeting.

The dog almost knocked him over as he jumped up onto him, licking Marcus's hands and face as he stooped over to rub behind his ears.

"I love you, too, Baxter boy. Want to go for a walk?" He reached for the dog's leash on the nail beside the door and snapped it onto his collar. "We'll go down to the park for a little while. Would you like that?"

As they went out the door, Baxter barked twice and then retrieved the half chewed-up Frisbee from the bottom step. He pulled against the leash as Marcus attempted to lock the door.

"Okay, okay, boy. I'm coming. Settle down, now." Marcus bent over to pat his faithful friend on top of his head. He regretted that it had been so long since he'd walked him. "Girls take up way too much time, don't they, Baxter?" If he kept reminding himself of that fact, maybe he wouldn't miss Sally so much.

It was amazing to him that he would even want her company after she'd treated him so badly last week. But he knew that if she'd ever show up at his house again, he'd welcome her back—apology or not. His mind replayed one of his favorite scenes from Spider-Man where Peter Parker looks longingly into Mary Jane's eyes. *Is this what love feels like?*

As they reached the park, Marcus threw the Frisbee across the thick carpet of grass. Baxter snagged it mid-air. "That'a boy!" Maybe he was an old dog, but he could still fetch as well as he did when he was a pup. They played for the better part of an hour before heading home. It was almost dark when Marcus turned his key in the lock. Baxter visited his water dish, curled up on his pillow and went promptly to sleep.

Marcus picked up the envelope he'd left in the middle of the kitchen table and slid his finger under the flap. He pulled out several sheets of lined yellow paper with bold writing scrawled across them in heavy black marker. Off in the margin, someone had drawn disturbing pictures: a knife with dripping blood, a headstone with *R.I.P.* on it, and a skull with crossbones. *What in the world?*

Dizziness overwhelmed him. He dropped into his chair, leaning over to rest his chin on the table. A minute later, he raised his head, forcing himself to read:

Marcus,

Here I am and there you are. I am in and you are out, but make no mistake about it, I still have friends that are more than willing to do favors for me.

I heard some pretty disturbing news from some of them.

They say you are spending a lot of time with Sally. You know she is my girl, right? She's having my baby.

I took the fall for both of us, Marcus. And this is the way you thank me?

You'd better do some hard thinking about this and cut all ties with Sally. You don't want to be the cause of you both getting hurt, do you?

Sally just needed a place to stay. She was never interested in you.

Simon

Chapter Eleven

It hurt. A lot.

Pastor Brice had prayed with Marcus this morning after he weeded, trimmed, and watered the prayer garden. Afterward, he had felt better—closer to God. But could *even God* heal his broken heart?

He hosed off the driveway and coiled the hose around the spigot at the side of his house. He felt like such a fool. Used by Sally. He'd learned to keep years of hurt feelings shoved down deep inside where they'd formed a shell around his heart. However, this time was different. He'd let Sally in.

He took Simon's letter from his pocket and read it once more. Even though he knew Simon was a liar and a bully, he nodded in agreement when he reread the last line. It was the truth. Sally hadn't had anywhere else to go, so she'd stayed with Marcus. In his need to feel accepted—and out of loneliness for Mama—he'd trusted her with his heart. Oh, he hadn't intended to...couldn't even pinpoint when it happened. The feeling had just suddenly bloomed like the flowers on Mama's rosebush.

He walked up the porch steps. It was an hour before lunch. Time enough for a nice long walk with Baxter before it got too hot. It had been over ninety degrees for several weeks now.

Angry voices from Betty's house captured his attention. Marcus paused and cocked his head. He walked toward the corner and stopped next to the hedge separating the driveway and the rest of the yard. *They're fighting again...*

"You're stupid, woman. You're just asking for trouble if you let that girl move in," Simon's father yelled as he threw a small suitcase into the trunk of his car.

"She's having a baby. She's no place to go." Betty wiped her tears with her checkered apron.

"That's no concern of ours." He rushed past her into the house.

Marcus stepped back into the shadow of the Palo Verde. They had to be talking about Sally. *Was she the reason Betty's husband was leaving?*

Mr. Wilson emerged from the house with an armload of clothes on hangers and threw them into the back seat. He slammed the car door and turned toward Betty. He took off his ball cap, scratched his head, and then replaced it. "Looks like you're finally going to get rid of me. We never were any good together anyhow. You can't cook a decent meal or get a job worth paying your keep. I was only waiting to leave until Simon graduated. And it's obvious that will never happen."

Betty bent over, clasping her folded arms to her chest, tears still flowing. "I was a good wife to you, but you never appreciated anything I did. Nothing ever pleased you. You took every problem at work or home out on me. I'll welcome the peace and quiet."

He spit into the grass, then turned and started toward her. "Peace and quiet? With a baby underfoot?"

Betty took a step backward. "Like it, or not, that baby will be our grandchild."

"*Your* grandchild. I want nothing to do with it. This is the last you'll ever see of me." He slid into the front seat, turned the key in the ignition, and backed out of the driveway. The car backfired as it headed down the street and out of sight.

Marcus's heartbeat was still pounding in his ears as he watched Betty walk back inside her house and close the door. He fought the urge to run over and comfort her, like he would have Mama. But he didn't want Betty to know he'd heard all that had gone on between her and Mr. Wilson. He decided on a silent prayer, instead. *God, please keep Betty safe and give her the peaceful life she deserves.*

Simon's father was unbelievable—and so much like Marcus's own father that it was shocking. Leaving because of a poor, helpless baby. Lincoln had left Mama all alone, too…

Lost in his own thoughts, he hadn't noticed a car as it pulled into the driveway. He was startled to hear Lincoln's voice. *Speak of the—*

"Hey, has the sun gotten to you? What are you doing out here without a hat?" Lincoln walked toward Marcus, shaking his head.

"No. I'm just...oh, it's hard to explain." Marcus shrugged, shielding his eyes as he looked up at his father.

Lincoln cleared his throat. "I've brought someone to meet you, Marcus."

"Oh?" Marcus turned in the direction of the car as its door opened and a smiling teenage boy with sandy brown hair and brown eyes stepped out.

"Mike, meet Marcus. Marcus, this is your half-brother, Mike."

Mike walked forward and grabbed Marcus in a bear hug that nearly squeezed the life out of him. "It's great to meet you. Jeff had tutoring, or he'd have come, too. He can hardly wait to see you for himself."

A lump formed in Marcus's throat. He felt dizzy and put his hand against the house to keep from falling.

"I can see now that I should have told you we were coming. Sorry, we just kind of sprung this on you. We just decided to drive up last night. We hopped in the car this morning and made a beeline for here. Mike has been so excited." Lincoln put an arm around Mike's shoulders and led him up the front steps. "All right if we come in and visit for a little bit?"

"Sh—sure." Marcus nodded and held the door open for them. "The living room is this way, Mike."

Baxter, napping at the end of the sofa, woke and barked a greeting. Tail wagging, he jumped up to be petted by Mike.

"You must be Baxter. Dad says you're twenty, but for an old guy you're looking good." Mike picked him up and nuzzled him. "Yeah, you're a good old boy, aren't you?"

Marcus took a seat in Mama's rocker, pointing his guests toward the couch. He rubbed his sweaty hands on the front of his jeans. *Were they really here?* He studied his brother's face as he talked. It was like looking at a better—more handsome—version of himself.

"I'm really glad to meet you. I can't believe I have another brother. I've always had Jeff to look up to, and now I'll have you, too. You're seventeen, right? When's your birthday?" Mike's slow smile grew bigger as he talked. His eyes twinkled with excitement.

Marcus leaned forward, resting his elbows on his knees. "I'll be eighteen July first. How old are you?"

"I'm almost sixteen. I'll be driving soon. I'm going to have my first lesson next weekend. Right, Dad?" Mike raised his eyebrows as he nodded in Lincoln's direction.

"Sure. And I, for one, will be glad when Mom and I don't have to spend most of our time hauling you boys back and forth." He reached over and playfully pulled the brim of Mike's cowboy hat down over his eyes.

"You watch it, old man." Mike started to go for his father's hat, but Lincoln deflected, grabbed his wrist and pulled his arm behind his back.

"Hey, let go." Mike laughed and jerked free.

Marcus couldn't help but be entertained by the loving back and forth banter between Mike and their father. Did he dare hope that someday Lincoln might feel the same way about him? He averted his eyes, studying the patterned rug under his feet. *Where did that thought come from, anyway? I don't care one iota about him.*

The warm shower felt good. As he squirted shampoo onto his hair, Marcus relived the events of the day—the fight between the Wilsons, his unexpected meeting with Mike. He shook his head and then pinched his arm with soapy fingers. Yep. He was awake. It hadn't been a dream after all.

As he rinsed off, he realized that he was really looking forward to meeting Jeff, too. All he knew about him was that he, at age nineteen, was the oldest of the three "brothers."

He towel-dried and dressed in his cut-off jeans and a clean T-shirt. "Okay, Baxter, let's go for our evening walk."

Baxter retrieved the Frisbee and was waiting by the front door by the time Marcus got the leash from the hook and his keys from the bowl in the center of the kitchen table.

As they rounded the hedge, Marcus almost ran into Sally. He jerked Baxter back and stood, frozen to the spot. "Sorry."

Sally's eyes brightened, but she didn't smile. "It's okay."

After a few awkward moments, Sally cleared her throat. "I was just going next—"

"Okay, sure. We're headed for a walk, so..." Marcus blinked when he noticed just how much Sally had grown in two weeks. "Are you having the baby soon?"

"In about four months. I'm showing now, huh?"

"Yeah. You sure are." Marcus winced. "You're still real pretty, though."

As Sally laughed, her lips curled into a genuine smile. "Thank you for the compliment." She grimaced as a yellow Mustang slowed in front of the house.

"I've got to go." She fled to Betty's door and knocked, repeatedly, until the door swung open.

Marcus shoved his hands into his back pockets as he watched her disappear into the house and the car pull away from the curb.

One of Simon's friends...

Marcus brought the garbage can around to the front of the house and flipped back the lid. The house had been T.P.'d overnight. What a mess. Toilet paper was strewn all over the hedge, trees, and planters. He went back to the garage for the ladder, set it under the largest of the palm trees, and climbed to the top.

He'd spent the night at Frannie's. If he'd been home, he surely would have heard them. They had to have been here for a long time because they had wound the toilet paper around the trees and even wrapped the fronds in it. They'd sprayed it all down with water when they were finished. He used the blunt end of a screwdriver to dig bits of wet toilet paper out of the bark. He frowned. He had better things to be doing on a Sunday morning than cleaning up a mess like this. He had just enough time to shower and head for church.

The phone was ringing as he stepped into the house. "Hello."

"Enjoy the additional yard work this morning?"

"Who is this?"

"Keep away from Sally. Consider this a warning. Don't let there be a next time, punk." The phone went dead.

Just as Marcus replaced the receiver, it rang again. "Leave me alone."

"Marcus?"

"Yes."

"Hey, it's Mike."

"Oh. Hi, Mike. How are you?"

"I'm great. Is anything wrong there? I assume you weren't telling me to leave you alone."

"No. I'm all right. Just some jerk with a wrong number."

"Hey, I have something I'd like you to think about."

"Sure."

"How would you like to learn to drive? Dad mentioned that you have your mother's car gathering dust in your garage, so I was thinking—"

"The answer is yes. I don't have to think about it." *Drive a car? Not have to take a bicycle or walk everywhere? Having a brother is turning out to be so cool.*

"All right, then. Dad and I will be there next Saturday morning for our first driving lesson."

"Will you bring Jeff?"

"No. He has another tutoring session. Anyway, he'd be bored while we have all the fun. He'll come to see you soon, though, I promise."

Marcus hung up the phone. He was going to learn to drive a car. In a million years, he would not have thought it possible. But then all kinds of impossible things seemed to be happening, lately.

Marcus sipped on an ICEE from Circle K as he walked home from church. The sermon had been about David's blessing from God. Marcus decided that he, too, was going to look at the good things that were happening to him as blessings from God. And, just like the pastor had said, he'd count them one by one—his brothers, Sally moving in with Betty, his driving lessons—and he'd thank God every day for his home and a mother who had saved enough money to provide him with the basics long after she'd gone to heaven.

As he approached his house, he heard Betty and Sally laughing and talking. They were standing under Betty's carport, tools scattered all over, and reading what looked to be a map or directions to something.

"I'll help you when I get home from work. I'm sure we can figure it out." Betty hopped onto Simon's bicycle and wobbled down the street.

Marcus paused, looking in both directions. The coast was clear. He walked next door. "Hi. Need some help?"

Sally's deep green eyes met his. "No, thank you." She turned her attention back to reading directions from the instruction booklet. "Put washer N onto bolt A. Insert in hole D. Now, where is that bolt?"

"Here." Marcus picked it up and handed it to her. "What are you trying to make?"

"A crib. Now, please go away, Marcus." Sally busied herself with finding the needed parts.

"You know, if I helped you carry those things to the back yard, we could put it together without anyone watching us." Marcus raised his eyebrows. "How about it?"

Sally looked in one direction, and then the other. She nodded, slowly. "I get it. Sure. Yeah, I guess so."

Marcus unlatched Betty's side gate and propped it open with a rock from their desert landscape. He spent the next few minutes carrying sections of the baby's bed to the back while Sally napped in a webbed lounge chair. He replaced the tools into the toolbox and carried it through the gate. He had already started on the project before Sally sat up and stretched.

"Marcus, would you mind giving me a hand? I can't seem to get myself out of this chair." Sally raised both arms toward him.

Marcus walked over, put his hands under Sally's arms and boosted her up. "You'd better stop eating so much. You're getting fat."

"Hasn't anyone ever told you not to say that to a girl?"

"No. Just ugly. And I didn't say you were ugly."

"Well, thanks for that." Sally laughed until her cheeks turned bright red. "Would you like some lemonade? Betty made it before she left."

"Okay. But you *are* going to help with this, aren't you?" Marcus gestured to the crib pieces strewn across the patio.

"Yes, of course." The screen smacked closed as she walked into the house.

"Right." Marcus said to himself and chuckled. His mother was the only woman he'd ever known to use more than a hammer or a screwdriver. Gramps had taught her. She had told Marcus she'd been a regular tomboy until she was a teenager.

Sally emerged from the house and thrust a cold glass into his hands. "I put lots of ice in it—and plenty of sugar." She paused. "Yoo-hoo, earth to Marcus. You were daydreaming."

"Sorry. I was thinking about Mama." He drained the glass; then placed it on the redwood picnic table.

"Your mom was really nice. No wonder you miss her. I think a mother is the most important person in a child's life. I'm going to be the best one I can possibly be."

"So, you've decided to keep it? Not have an abortion, I mean?"

Sally rolled her eyes. "Didn't the fact that we're assembling a crib give you a hint?"

"Yeah, huh?" Marcus hit the side of his forehead with the heel of his hand. "I'm glad to hear it."

Sally took a sip of lemonade. "I just hope Simon feels that way."

"What do you mean?"

"He's been pretty firm about not wanting to be a father."

"My dad didn't want to be one, either—well, at least not to me. The only reason I ever even met him was because Mama made him my guardian." Marcus pinched his eyes shut and then lowered his head into his hands. His shoulders shook as he cried, words sandwiched between sobs. "Pretty rotten, isn't it? Mama had to die in order for Lincoln to finally show his face around here."

Sally set her glass on the table next to his and then wound her arms around Marcus's waist. "I'm so sorry. Looks like fathers are just a bad bunch all the way around."

Marcus melted into her embrace. He sighed, imagining she was Mama, holding him gently as he poured out his heart like he had so many times over the years. Then he became acutely aware of Sally's closeness—her softness, the light fragrance in her hair, and the baby growing inside her as it kicked Marcus soundly in the ribs.

Chapter Twelve

All day Friday was spent washing and cleaning Mama's car inside and out. Sitting now in the first light of a much-anticipated Saturday morning, it sparkled like Marcus imagined it had more than a decade ago on the showroom floor. No wonder it had been his Gramp's pride and joy.

Marcus could hardly wait for his first driving lesson. He'd been studying the manual for the last few days, memorizing the rules, hand signals, and the meaning of all the warning signs. He didn't know exactly why, but something inside made him want to make Lincoln proud.

He let the screen door slam shut as he headed for the kitchen and his customary bowl of cereal. If they started out first thing, he figured Mike and Lincoln should arrive in about an hour. That would give him plenty of time to straighten up the house and clean the bathroom. He hoped no one would be coming to look at the house today, so their time together wouldn't be interrupted.

Once he was showered and the house cleaned, Marcus took Baxter for a quick walk around the neighborhood. Baxter gave the customary sniff test to several dogs along the way, drank from a broken fire hydrant, and greeted Sheila as she and her parents headed toward the park.

Sheila looked cute with her kite in hand, riding in her little red wagon next to a picnic basket. The wagon looked new. *Had she bought it with her Halloween money?*

Marcus was glued to the living room window by ten o'clock, but it was close to eleven o'clock before Lincoln pulled up in front of the house. Mike leaped out of the passenger door with a large pizza box. Lincoln followed with a six-pack of Coca Cola. He stopped to run his hand along the hood of the Impala before following Mike and Marcus into the house.

He came through the door, setting the sodas on the kitchen table. "The car looks good, Marcus. Did it start up all right?"

Marcus shrugged his shoulders. "I don't know."

Lincoln frowned. "What do you mean, you 'don't know'?"

"I just pushed it out of the garage. Mama said never to start it up."

Lincoln rolled his eyes, but then smiled. "Well, let's cross our fingers while we eat and hope for the best. If it doesn't start, we can use my car. I had just wanted you to get used to your own car. It's nice to learn how to drive both a stick and an automatic."

Mike slid the pizza box onto the table and Marcus poured ice and soda into tall plastic glasses. Mike caught the overflow off his glass with his tongue. "I've been excited all week. How about you?"

"It's been the longest week of my life. It's sure hard to wait for good things, isn't it?" Marcus swiped at the sauce accumulating on his chin.

"Yeah," Mike answered as he wolfed down a second piece of pizza.

Lincoln blocked Mike's hand when we reached for a third. "Slow down, Mike. That car's not going anywhere. Let's enjoy our lunch. Then, I'm going to quiz you on the rules of the road before we even leave the driveway. In fact, we have to go down to the DMV and have Marcus take his written test before he can get behind the wheel."

Marcus reached for the manual and handed it to Lincoln. "I've been studying all week. You can ask me anything. I mean it. Ask me anything you want. I know that book inside and out. You'll see."

Lincoln pushed back from the table and took the manual from Marcus's hand. "Okay. Let me see… what's the speed limit in a school zone?"

"Fifteen."

"If your blinker doesn't work, what should you do?"

"Use hand signals."

"That's right. Do you know the hand signals?"

Marcus responded with the signal for a right turn, left turn, and stop, followed by "the finger."

"That isn't funny, Marcus. Was that aimed toward me?"

Marcus's face reddened. "What do you mean?"

Lincoln put his hands on the table and pushed up, towering over Marcus with a scowl on his face. He raised his voice as he answered. "I mean, you'd better explain the exact meaning of that last hand signal." He sat back down, drumming his fingers on the table as he waited for Marcus to answer.

Marcus gulped. "It wasn't in the book, but I see guys using it all the time."

"Well, let's not use it again, okay? It's a sign some guys like to show in traffic when they're annoyed or irritated at another driver. It's rude and offensive. Understand?"

Marcus nodded his head. "I didn't know."

"Well, now that you do, I don't want to see you ever using that again. Right?"

"Right."

"Like I said, Mike took his written test Wednesday and got his permit. Let's get down to the DMV so you can take yours. Mike can drive there if we stay off the busiest streets. Then, coming back, you can have a turn. We'll look at your car when we get home. If it checks out all right, we can drive it next time."

Marcus bit his lip. He was stuck on the last question. He'd been staring at the drawing for the past five minutes. Four cars were waiting at a four-way stop. "Which car can go first?" he muttered to himself. He closed his eyes. *I need your help, God. I thought I knew*

everything. It was my own stubborn pride—just like in last week's sermon—that kept me from studying harder. Please clear my brain and help me figure this out. Amen.

He looked at the drawing once more, tracing the path of each car with his index finger. "C. That's got to be it." The chair scraped across the tile as he pushed back from the small desk. His hand shook as he presented his exam paper to the lady at the counter.

She continued her conversation with the guy at the next window as she swiped her black pen across two answers. She gave the test back to Marcus, pointing toward a long line on the other side of the room. As he walked in that direction, he held the paper high in the air—a banner of victory.

Mike sent him a thumbs-up. Then Lincoln joined him at the window, producing Marcus's birth certificate he'd picked up from Mama's safe deposit box. He signed the guardianship form and shoved it across the counter.

When the clerk gave Marcus his driver's permit, he whooped all the way to the car. With one hand, he snatched the keys that Lincoln sent flying through the air. He slid into the driver's seat with Lincoln taking his place on the passenger's side. He took a deep breath, turned the key in the ignition and drove semi-confidently toward home.

Approaching the driveway, Sally caught his attention as she walked toward Betty's mailbox. Her distraction was just enough to make Marcus misjudge the turn and hit the trashcan on the curb. Garbage spilled out, rolling in all directions.

Mike emerged from the car, laughing. "Wow, that was quite an initiation into the world of driving."

Marcus scowled as he walked toward the debris, his face hot.

Lincoln strode to the front of the car to assess the damage. "You're lucky it's not scratched. You need to keep your eyes—and your mind—on the road at all times. Now, hurry and get this mess cleaned up before someone calls the city and complains."

Lincoln pulled the car into the driveway while Marcus set the can upright. Mike helped him gather the spilled contents. Then Marcus hosed off the driveway.

The smell was enough to make Marcus gag, but he experienced a camaraderie between himself and Mike that was both new and exciting. "You didn't have to help me, you know."

"Hey, that's what brothers are for."

The following Saturday, Marcus hustled to do his own mowing, as well as Betty's, before noon. He'd been working off his debt to the Wilsons ever since he'd broken their car window. *How many years has it been, anyway? Long enough that I could have paid for a dozen windows, I'll bet.*

He had long ago become skeptical of Mr. Wilson stringing him along just to get out of doing his own yard work. However, Marcus had already decided to help Betty out each week until Mr. Wilson returned home—that is, if he ever did come back to his family. *Maybe a grandchild will make the difference…*

Today was Jeff's birthday. Mike and Lincoln had invited him along for the celebration. Marcus was excited to finally meet his other brother. He wondered if Jeff was anything like Mike.

As soon as Mike pulled their car into the driveway, Marcus was out the door and down the steps in a flash. His brother looked good behind the wheel. Maybe Marcus would get a turn later today after the birthday celebration.

Mike was the first one out of the car. Marcus gave him a big hug. "Where's Jeff?" Marcus pushed his head through the open car window. One good look at Jeff made his head spin. He backed away and turned to give Mike a quizzical look. *They could have prepared me for this...*

Jeff slid out of the car with a huge grin on his face. "Mar—Marc. Brubber." He gave him a bear hug that almost cut off his air supply.

"Jeff, let go of Marcus. He's turning blue." Lincoln pried Jeff's pudgy hands loose from Marcus's neck. "Sorry. He's just excited. You okay?"

Marcus cracked his neck as he turned it from side to side. "Yeah, I guess so."

He started for the house, calling back over his shoulder. "I'm j—just going to g—get a jacket and lock the door. Mike, can I see you for a minute?"

Mike followed him inside, shutting the door behind him. "What's up?"

"Why didn't you guys tell me about Jeff—I mean how he is and all?"

"I thought Dad told you." He paused, biting his lower lip. "Does it matter to you?"

"No. He seems friendly—great, really. It was just a surprise. That's all."

When they heard the car horn beep, Mike stuck his head outside the door. "Just a minute. We'll be right out." He turned back to Marcus. "Are you sure Dad didn't tell you?"

"I'm sure."

"Well, he can explain better than me, but when he married Mom, she already had Jeff. He's retarded. Oh, don't get me wrong. He's a great brother. We all love him, including Dad. He spends a lot of time with him. I'm sure Dad thinks of him as his own son."

Marcus could feel the anger he'd stuffed down for so long threatening to surface. He balled his fists at his side.

"What's the matter?"

Marcus paused. Should he share his feelings? Would Mike stand up for his father? "Nothing against Jeff, but Lincoln left me when I was born. I was his very own son. But then he goes and raises somebody else's kid and treats him special and all. How do you think that makes *me* feel?"

"I know." Mike put his arm around Marcus's shoulders. "It's bad. I don't understand it, either. But this is between you and Dad. The two of you need to talk and settle this. That's for sure. But Jeff and I really don't have anything to do with it. Can we just set this aside for this one afternoon and all go out and have a good time together?"

"I don't feel like going anymore."

"Please, Marcus, do this for me. Do this for Jeff. He's really a great kid. I know you'll agree when you get to know him. I'm excited to have you and him finally get together. Please."

Marcus slipped on his navy and red plaid jacket and switched off the light. "I'll try. You sit up front, though. I'll sit in the back with Jeff."

Mike mussed Marcus's hair. "Thanks. We'll have a great time. You'll see. By the way, don't you think 'Marcus' is a little formal?"

"What do you mean?"

"Well, I'm Michael, but they call me Mike. Jeff is short for Jeffrey. So, what do you think about us calling you Marc?"

His heart swelled with pride. *A nickname. Who would've ever thought?* "Cool."

Sweat ran down his forehead and stung as it dripped into Marcus's eyes. He turned the wheel hard to the right and rammed into Jeff's yellow bumper car for the third time.

In less than a second, Mike hit Marcus's blue torpedo from behind.

"Hey, watch it, Mike. You're next." He'd never had such a good time. Nothing even remotely compared to this day. He sure was glad he'd put his feelings for Lincoln aside and come with them.

"Hey, guys, you can keep driving if you want to, but I'm going to sit under the awning over there and cool off. This is way too much activity for an old guy like me." Lincoln vacated his bumper car and headed toward the refreshment stand.

A few minutes later, Marcus yelled to Mike. "Hey, you get on the left side of Jeff and I'll ram him from the right." Marcus pulled his car into position and pressed the pedal all the way down to the floorboard.

Mike followed suit, broad siding Jeff at the same instant that Marcus hit from the right. Jeff's car started to smoke and then sputtered to a stop.

All three boys laughed so hard they had tears in their eyes as they climbed out of their cars. Mike and Jeff flanked Marcus, putting their arms over his shoulders as they walked toward Lincoln. "Here come the three Amigos!"

All of a sudden, Jeff slumped and fell into the soft green grass. He gasped for breath as sweat beaded on his upper lip.

Lincoln rushed across the lawn, pulled an inhaler from his pocket and administered a couple of puffs. Jeff continued to wheeze as Lincoln slapped his cheeks and rubbed his hands and arms. "Will someone call an ambulance?"

Seconds later, Marcus heard the siren. He twisted his fingers as he stepped back to allow two medics to make their way through the crowd.

They put an oxygen mask on Jeff and placed him on a gurney. The taller of the two guys looked toward Lincoln. "He your son?"

"Y—yes."

"Asthma attack?"

"I think so, but the inhaler just didn't do the trick this time."

"Good thing you called us. You want to ride with him?"

"No. This is my son, Mike. Let him go along. My other boy and I will follow you in my car. What hospital?"

"Tempe Community. It's on Mill Avenue."

Mike hopped into the back of the ambulance with Jeff. The siren went on as soon as the doors shut.

Lincoln sprinted to his car, motioning for Marcus to keep up. They were both nearly out of breath as they reached it. Lincoln put the key in the ignition and turned to Marcus. "So much for our first guys' night out, huh?"

"We shouldn't have rammed him. It was my fault. It was my idea." Marcus turned his head to stare out the window.

"No. Don't think that. It's been breezy today, kicking up a lot of dust in the air. We probably shouldn't have done an outside activity. Poor planning on our part."

Marcus ran his fingers through his hair. He was able to open the car door and run for the edge of the parking lot before he heaved up the remains of a giant pretzel, snow cone, and cotton candy. His legs wobbled as he returned to the car.

"Put your head down between your legs and take some deep breaths. Jeff will be fine."

Marcus's stomach continued to churn on the way to the hospital. He felt guilty for the part he had played in Jeff's asthma attack. He really liked his brother and the thought of losing him before they really had a chance to know each other was what scared him the most. *God, please don't take Jeff away from me. I figure we are all together for a reason—maybe to help me not be so lonely for Mama. Please spare him and teach me how to be a good brother.*

Lincoln parked in the emergency parking lot. As they headed toward the double doors to the ER, he put his hand on Marcus's arm. "Come on, son."

A chill went through his body. Marcus rejoiced at being called *son*, but part of him also wanted to pull away from this man who dared to call himself his father. *What's wrong with me? After all, isn't this what I've always wanted?*

Chapter Thirteen

The ringing of the phone roused Marcus from a deep sleep. He rolled over to look at the time on the digital alarm clock on his dresser. Seven o'clock. *Who would be calling me this early?* He threw back the sheet and stumbled across the bedroom floor, down the hall, and grabbed the phone from the kitchen wall. "Hello?"

"Marcus, this is—this is—ouch—Sally." Her frantic cries were followed by heavy breathing.

"What's wrong?" He could hear the pain—and fear—in her voice. *What could have happened?* His heart thumped wildly in his chest.

"I think I'm having the baby."

"Oh, congratulations."

"No, no, you don't—oh, dear God—understand. I've got to get to the hospital and Betty has already left for work. The baby isn't due until next month. That's four weeks early..."

Marcus slumped into a chair at the kitchen table. "What do you want me to do? Call the doctor?" He waited for a response, but when none came, he bolted from the chair and ran barefoot next door. He rang the bell several times, but when Sally didn't answer, he opened the gate to the backyard and entered the house through the unlocked patio door.

Sally was sitting on the floor against the kitchen wall, doubled over. Relief swept over her face when she saw Marcus. She lifted her arms and reached toward him. "Thank goodness. Marcus, help me up."

He put his hands under her arms and pulled her to her feet. "Here you go."

Sally placed the palm of her hand against the wall to steady herself. "Go get your car. You've got to drive me. And hurry. See all that water on the floor? That's from the baby."

"How could a baby do that? I've never heard—"

"Marcus!" Sally yanked on the neck of his T-shirt. "Don't worry about it now. Just go get the car." Sally blew out a strong breath that lifted the bangs off her forehead. "Hurry."

"I don't have my license yet, Sal—"

"Marcus, listen. This is an emergency. It doesn't count. You won't get in trouble. Just get the car."

He hesitated. "Okay, if you're sure."

Sally took a deep breath and then gritted her teeth. "I am, Marcus. Just do it."

Marcus raced out of the house, across the side yard, and into the house. He grabbed the keys from the middle of the table and started out the door. When he saw himself in the hallway mirror, he stopped. He couldn't go to the hospital in his P.J.'s.

Leaving the door open, he turned toward the bedroom. He changed into his Sunday pants and best shirt. He was slipping his feet into his loafers when Sally appeared in the doorway.

"What are you doing?" Sally questioned just before she grabbed onto the doorframe for support. "Ouch."

"I had to get dressed. Don't you want me to—?"

"Get the keys. Let's go. NOW." Sally stumbled out the door and headed around the side of the house toward the garage.

Marcus followed, raised the wooden door, and helped Sally into the back seat. He turned on the ignition. "I haven't had my backing out lesson yet. I—"

Sally pulled herself to a sitting position. "Marcus, put it in reverse. See that *R*, there? That will make it go backward. Watch where you're going and stop when we get into the street. Then, put it in *D* for drive. Quick, Marcus, quick."

Marcus nodded and put the car in reverse, stopping to put it into drive when it cleared the driveway. He grinned. "I did it."

"Good," Sally answered between breaths. "Head toward the hospital."

"Uh, where is it?" Marcus turned around to look into the back seat when Sally didn't answer.

She stared at him, tears filling her eyes. "You don't know?"

He laughed nervously. "Of course, I do. Just kidding."

"That's not funny, Marcus." She let her head fall back against the seat.

Marcus knew a short cut to Tempe Community through two neighborhoods. He hit a scooter left unattended on the sidewalk but less than ten minutes later, they arrived without further incident at the emergency entrance. He leaped from the car, opened the door, and ran inside. "Help! Sally's having the baby," he yelled toward the nurse at the desk.

From that point on, there was a flurry of activity. A nurse got Sally out of the car and into a wheelchair. Marcus followed as she was carted down a hallway with a stork painted on the wall. It was carrying a bag of some sort in his beak.

"Are you the father?" The nurse asked as she waited for the double doors to open.

"No. I—"

"Then, just take a seat over there," she said, pointing to a row of chairs against the waiting room wall. "I'll be back in a little while." The doors closed behind them with a whoosh.

Marcus lowered himself into one of the bright orange vinyl chairs and looked at his Spider-Man watch. Eight o'clock. He was drained of all energy. He laid his head back against the wall and closed his eyes. *Please, God, let the baby be born okay and please be with Sally. I know she's scared.*

Betty and Marcus stood in front of the glass windows of the hospital nursery looking at the small bundle in the nurse's arms. They both waved and made goo-goo faces at Betty's granddaughter for a few minutes before the nurse put her back in a bassinette and drew the blinds closed.

Marcus turned to Betty. "She sure is little—and kind of ugly, too. You won't tell Sally I said that, though, will you?" Marcus raised his eyebrows in Betty's direction.

She laughed and shook her head. "No. I won't. Most babies look all wrinkled for the first day or so. By tomorrow, she'll look beautiful."

"What do you think Sally will name her?" Marcus asked as they returned to the waiting room.

"I'm not sure. That's something for you to ask Sally." Betty gave Marcus's hand a pat. "I've got to get back to work now. Tell the new mama I'll be back around suppertime. You should go home and get some rest after your visit. She'll probably want you to call her mother. I'll get word to Simon."

"Okay, Betty." Marcus watched her as she left. Then he walked down the hall toward the small gift shop he'd seen earlier when he'd gone to the cafeteria for lunch. He'd noticed people with balloons, flowers, and wrapped gifts coming and going all day. He wanted to get something special. *Maybe a stuffed animal?*

Marcus took his time looking at potted plants, flower arrangements, even charms for bracelets that could be engraved with the birth date and name of the baby. *Everything is so expensive.* He spotted a pair of eyes peeking out from behind a vase of roses. Reaching behind the flowers, he pulled out a small white lamb with a pink bow around its neck. *The baby would really like this.*

He placed it on the counter by the cash register and rang the bell. A minute later, a girl with a red and white striped uniform emerged from the back room. "Can I help you? Marcus?"

"Uh, oh, hi, Gidget." Marcus felt a flush travel up his neck to his face. The cute girl with brown curly hair went to the same high school. She was one of Sally's best friends.

She stared at the stuffed animal in his hands. "If you're here, that must mean Sally had her baby."

"Yeah, a little girl. She's just a few hours old." He thrust the toy into Gidget's outstretched hands. "How much is this lamb? I couldn't find a tag on it."

"Where was this little guy? I thought we'd sold all of our clearance toys."

Marcus pointed to the vase of flowers on the shelf. "Behind there."

"Well, it's your lucky day. He's only four dollars. Four dollars and eight cents, with tax."

"I'll take it," Marcus replied. He laid a five-dollar bill on the counter between them.

"Do you want it gift-wrapped?" she asked, handing back his change.

"No, that's okay. How's a baby going to unwrap a package, anyway?"

"Oh, Marcus, you're just too funny." Gidget doubled over, laughing. "What room is she in?"

"The nursery, silly."

Gidget shook her head. "I meant Sally."

"Oh, yeah." Marcus looked on the palm of his hand where he'd written the number in ink. "She's in 212."

"I can't wait to see the baby. I'll pop in on her when I go on break."

Marcus cocked his head to the side. "You work here?"

"Marcus, didn't I just sell you that lamb?"

"Yeah."

"Then, I must work here, huh?"

Marcus's face grew hot once more.

"I'm what they call a 'candy striper.' It's kind of like a volunteer—just for the summer, until school starts again."

"Oh."

They both stood, awkwardly, staring at each other until Marcus cleared his throat. "Well, I'd better be going. If you go to see Sally, don't wake her up. She needs lots of rest. It's hard work having a baby."

Gidget put her hands on her hips. "Well, you don't say. Who are you now, her bodyguard?"

"I'm just watching out for her, that's all."

"Don't go getting so possessive. One of these days Simon will get out. You don't want him misunderstanding your relationship with the mother of his child. That could cause big trouble. But I shouldn't have to tell you that."

"No. I know how it is."

She waggled her finger at him. "Just be sure you do. You're the only one who's going to get hurt in all of this, Marcus."

"Right." He turned slowly toward the door.

"See you around."

"Yeah. See ya." Marcus walked over to the elevator. He flicked the bell hanging from the ribbon around the lamb's neck. It made a slight tinkling sound. He was tempted to toss the toy into the trashcan nearby. Maybe Gidget was right. He shouldn't get involved with Sally. She'd already hurt him more than once.

When the elevator door opened on the second floor, Marcus found himself walking in the direction of the nursery. He couldn't see what harm there would be in helping her with the baby...

Sally was laughing when Marcus entered the room that afternoon. She was talking on the phone. "Oh, I miss you, too. I can't wait for you to see her. She weighed five pounds. They say that's surprisingly big for a preemie. She might have to stay in the hospital for a little while, but she's healthy and so, so beautiful."

She must be talking to Simon. A lump found its way into his throat. He suddenly felt sick to his stomach. Was that anger? Jealousy? He'd better get hold of himself. He didn't want Sally to know how he felt. And just how was that? He didn't even know himself. But just hearing her talk so sweet to Simon on the phone made Marcus want to puke. Who was he to call her, anyway?

Oh, yeah, he was the father.

"Marcus, what do you have there?" Sally asked after she hung up the phone. "Come here. Let me see."

Marcus approached the bed, handing her the soft toy that smelled faintly of baby powder. "How are you feeling?"

"Amazing."

"Really?"

"No. I hurt. I could hardly walk to the bathroom and back a few minutes ago."

Marcus studied her face as she snuggled the toy's softness next to her cheek. "Mary had a little lamb."

Her eyes gleamed as she clapped the palm of her hand to her cheek. "That's it. You've helped me name the baby. I'm going to name her Mary."

Marcus felt his heart flutter. He couldn't help but smile. "It's a perfect name."

"I think so, too. And it was sweet of you to buy her first toy." Sally pushed herself up and planted a soft kiss on his cheek. "Thanks for getting me to the hospital this morning and making sure I was all right. When I was having the baby, all I could see was your face when you were putting the crib together and when you were joking about not knowing how to get to the hospital. That's what got me through it. I just kept seeing your smile and I, well—"

"What?"

"Oh, nothing. You're just the best friend ever. I mean that. No one else could ever come close." Her luminous eyes held his for the briefest of moments before she cleared her throat and turned her attention to the bassinette as it was being wheeled into the room.

Her face radiated love and happiness as the nurse placed Mary into her arms. She traced the baby's lips with her forefinger and then kissed her nose and her forehead. "She even has hair, Marcus. It's so soft."

Marcus stroked the fuzz on the baby's head. "Can I hold her?"

"Have you ever held a baby before?"

"Oh, sure. Lots of times." Not really, but how hard could it be?

"Okay, then." Sally placed the baby in his arms. "She's looking right at you, Marcus. She'll know you in no time at all."

Marcus brushed the baby's fingers with his own. "She's perfect. She looks just like her mama."

"You think so?"

"I sure do. The boys are going to be falling all over themselves just to be near her."

"That's years from now. I'm going to have her all to myself for a long, long time."

"Me, too. I want to be part of her life—I mean, can I?" Marcus couldn't take his eyes off of the baby. This small little bit of life was precious to him already.

"Of course. You helped name her, after all."

Who would have known that a baby could make such a profound change in his outlook? In an instant he knew that there was nothing he wouldn't do for this little girl.

Marcus dropped into bed with his clothes on and his stomach growling. He was too tired to even fix himself a sandwich. After he left the hospital, he'd gone by Sally's parents' home to give them the news. He thought for a moment that he'd seen a glimmer of caring in Mrs. Schwartz's eyes. Had he been imagining it?

Poor Sally. Friends were great, but she needed family, too. Maybe someday they'd change their minds and welcome her back into their lives. Until then, Marcus would be there for her—and, of course, there was Betty. They'd be her family—her support—in the days ahead.

A light shone across his bedroom the way it used to when Mr. Wilson pulled into his driveway next door after working the night shift. *Oh, surely not. What's he up to?*

Marcus rolled off the bed and bent the blinds down with his forefinger. He peered outside to see Mr. Wilson's car parked in his driveway. His eyes roved over the sidewalk and yard, finally coming to rest on his silhouette pounding on the front door, cupping his hands at the living room window and trying to see inside the darkened house.

Maybe he forgot something when he moved out. Maybe he was coming back to apologize to Betty. Maybe—No, Marcus knew it wouldn't do any good for him to speculate. In all these years that the Wilsons had been their neighbors, Marcus had never been able to figure that man out—his loud mouth...his temper...his hatred of his own son.

Mr. Wilson walked a few steps toward his car and then paused. He turned toward Marcus's house, scratched his head, and then marched up the sidewalk with determination, his huge arms swinging close to his body. Had he spotted Marcus at the window?

The repeated knocking at the front door caused his pulse to quicken. He covered his ears, willing the man to go away and leave their neighborhood in peace.

Marcus grabbed Baxter from the foot of the bed, sprinted to the back of the house, and opened the door to Mama's bedroom. Locking it behind him, he slipped inside the closet. He crouched on the floor, hid behind Mama's rose-colored robe and rested his elbow on her fluffy slippers.

It was then that he heard the breaking of glass, followed moments later by loud footsteps in the hall.

Chapter Fourteen

"I know you're in there, you little snot."

Marcus cringed at the words Mr. Wilson shouted through the bedroom door. What could he do? The man was twice his size and had probably been drinking. He put his hand over Baxter's muzzle when he started to whimper. "Shhh."

"Marcus, come out and talk to me. All I want is to know where my wife is at this time of night. She should be home in bed—where all decent women are. Does she have a boyfriend? Answer me, you piece of trash."

The crack of wood breaking was immediately followed by heavy breathing just outside the closet door. Marcus's heart raced as the brass doorknob slowly turned and a large hand reached between two of Mama's dresses and found its way around his throat. He squirmed and coughed as Mr. Wilson dragged him from his hiding place.

Baxter fell out of his arms and onto the floor. He clamped his teeth onto the cuff of Mr. Wilson's pants, growling as he tugged.

"Get away, you mongrel." Mr. Wilson kicked at the dog. "Better call him off, Marcus, or I'll kill him. I swear I will."

"No way. I'll—"

Baxter let out a single *yelp* when Mr. Wilson's boot came down hard on his back. Then he fell silent.

With a surge of energy, Marcus tore himself from the man's grip, pushed him aside, and scooped up Baxter. He fled down the hall and through the kitchen in giant strides. He threw open the back door, nearly tripping over the lawn mower as he bounded through the gate and into the dark alley. He shook the dog, gently. "You're going to be all right. Sure, you are. Baxter, wake up. Come on, boy."

Marcus cried out in pain as bits of metal and broken glass embedded themselves in the soles of his bare feet. He bit his bottom lip, hobbling on one foot and then the other as he neared the end of the alley. He turned right and headed toward Frannie's house. Streetlights cast eerie shadows on the long stretch of sidewalk ahead. He stopped for a moment, eyes darting in both directions. The street was clear. No sign of Mr. Wilson. He let out a long breath.

Tears trickled down his cheeks as he inched forward. Each excruciating step left bloody tracks on the cold sidewalk. He brought Baxter's lifeless body up to his face, kissing him over and over again. "Please, please, God. Let him be okay."

Rounding the corner, the white picket fence surrounding Frannie's house came into view. He forged ahead, collapsing when he reached the steps. The light from the living room window shined like a beacon of hope. Marcus reached up and pounded against the doorframe.

When the outside light came on, Marcus sent up a prayer of thanks.

Floyd opened the door, gasping when his attention fell on Marcus—half sitting, half lying at the top of the steps—just inches away. "Whoa. What's happened, Marcus?" He stepped outside and squatted down beside him.

"It's—it's Baxter. He's hurt bad." He looked down at the limp form in his arms.

"Let's get him inside and take a look." Floyd opened the door wide.

Marcus raised Baxter up, his arms quivering. "Here. Take him."

"What's wrong? You hurt, too?"

"I stepped on something. I can't walk."

Floyd took Baxter from Marcus. "I'll be back in a minute." He ran inside with the dog. "Frannie, wake up. Marcus needs us," Floyd shouted over his shoulder, the screen door slamming behind him.

A few minutes later, Frannie stumbled out the door, pulling her plush white robe around her and knotting its wide sash at her waist. "What's happened, dear?" She circled around Marcus and sat down beside him on the steps. She gasped when she saw his bloody feet. "Oh, Dear Lord Jesus. What have you done, Marcus?"

"I was trying to get away from Mr. Wilson. I was already in bed when he came home—to his house, I mean. He must've seen me at the window. He just went berserk."

"That man has been nothing but trouble for years. Such anger there, you know. But let's get you inside and Baxter taken care of—I'm sure that's another story. Floyd will know what to do. I bet you didn't know he was a veterinarian for forty years before he retired, did you?"

"No. I mean yes. I mean, I didn't know about him being a veterinarian, but something just told me, clear as could be, that I needed to bring Baxter *here*."

"Not something. *Someone*. Divine intervention. That's what I'd call it."

Marcus nodded. "I learned about it at church. It means God led me here."

"Yes, I believe He did." She held the door open wide. "Now, let's see if you can scoot yourself into the house so I can take a look at your feet while Floyd tends to Baxter."

"Ouch. Ouch." Marcus bit the back of his hand to keep from crying.

"These shots in the soles of your feet are necessary, son. If I didn't deaden the nerves, you'd never let me in there to clean them. Believe me, this is a lot less painful than the alternative." The doctor put the cap on the needle and rolled his stool away from the examining table. He rested his back against the wall, writing on a clipboard in short chicken scratches. "I've tried to get my own kids to stop going barefoot. I've warned them about this sort of thing happening to them."

"I didn't have a choice. A guy was chasing me. He hurt my dog." Marcus swiped at his runny nose with the back of his hand.

"I heard about that from the lady that brought you in. That's really tough." He dropped a small white pill onto the palm of Marcus's hand and gave him a paper cup filled with water. "This will calm you down… maybe make you a little woozy. But when it works its magic, we'll be able to fix you up good as new." The doctor headed for the door, turning to wink in his direction. "Give that a few minutes and I'll be back."

Marcus laid his head against the small pillow at the end of the examining table and let his eyelids flutter closed. After a night of no sleep, he welcomed a chance to catnap. His thoughts turned to Mama, his brothers, Lincoln, Pastor Brice, and finally Sally and baby Mary. Would Sally bring the baby home today? Would Mr. Wilson try to hurt them, too? *I need to warn them.* He was struggling to sit up when the doctor returned, his nurse following him into the room.

"Hey, buddy. Let's lay back and get this over with, all right? Anything you've got going today will wait until later." The doctor pointed his chin toward the head of the table, signaling the nurse to stand next to Marcus.

When she touched his shoulders, Marcus shook her off. "Gotta go. Gotta tell Sally—"

"Come on, now, Marcus. Work with us. You don't want us to have to put you completely out, do you, son?" The doctor rolled a stool into position at the foot of the table, picked up an instrument and took hold of Marcus's right foot. "Tell me if you can feel anything."

Marcus took a deep breath, allowing the medication to overtake his senses and send him adrift in a soft, fuzzy world for the next few minutes. The next thing he remembered was the nurse helping him into a wheelchair and propping up his bandaged feet. She placed a curved plastic container into his hands. "Sometimes patients get an upset stomach from that medicine."

Marcus stared at the dish and nodded. Mama had been sick on medication after her operation, too.

The nurse wheeled him back into the waiting room, where Pastor Brice was engrossed in reading a magazine. "Just in time for a friend to take you out to lunch."

"Oh, I'm not hungry." He turned to the Pastor. "Thanks for coming. Frannie had to get to work and Floyd had an appointment. I didn't know who else to call."

"No problem, but does that mean you're not going to weed the prayer garden today?" His solemn face turned into a broad grin. "Just kidding."

"He needs to stay off those feet for a few days, if possible. And by the way, there's an outstanding bill. Are you the one to talk to about that?" The nurse gave Marcus's shoulders a pat. "Don't worry. Things will work out for the best," she whispered.

Pastor Brice took the charge slip from the nurse's hand. "I'll see this gets taken care of."

He turned to Marcus. "Anywhere you need to go on the way home?"

"Dairy Queen?"

"I thought you said you weren't hungry."

"I'm not."

Marcus waited in the car while Pastor Brice retrieved Baxter from the Western Pets Veterinary Office. Floyd had a veterinarian friend that owed him a favor. He said he'd take x-rays to see if the Schnauzer had any broken bones. Marcus watched as the pastor carried Baxter down the sidewalk and toward the car. The dog's midsection was wrapped in gauze between his front and hind legs.

When the pastor placed Baxter in his lap, Marcus gave him a gentle squeeze. "It's good to see you, boy. Look what I've got for you." He held the huge vanilla cone up to Baxter's mouth.

Marcus stroked his fur as he gobbled up his frozen treat.

The pastor pulled out of the parking lot and headed in the direction of Marcus's house.

"What did the vet say? Is Baxter going to be all right?"

"He said he has one cracked rib, which he taped up. He's an old dog, remember, so the less movement the better. No jumping. No Frisbee. He has an appointment for a follow up visit. Here's the card. Clip that to your calendar at home."

Marcus stuck the card in the pocket of his jeans. "Thanks for everything, Pastor."

He turned to Marcus. "Feel like telling me what happened to the two of you last night?"

"Mr. Wilson came over to the house looking for Betty. I knew she was probably at the hospital, but I wasn't going to tell him that. He stomped on Baxter when my little buddy tried to protect me. I ran through the alley to get away from him."

"Without shoes."

"Yeah."

Pastor Brice eased onto the street, carefully merging into the flow of traffic. He drove the last two blocks in silence, pulling into the driveway of Marcus's house behind Lincoln's Cadillac. "Looks like you've got company."

Jeff, Mike, and Lincoln were sitting in a row on the shady porch steps when the car pulled into the driveway. All three hopped up and rushed around to the passenger door.

Lincoln reached through the open window to shake hands with Pastor Brice. "Thanks. We appreciate you always being there for Marcus."

"No problem. He's in your good hands, now, so I'm just going to get on with my day."

Mike took Baxter from Marcus's arms and Jeff and Lincoln cradled Marcus in a makeshift sling, carrying him up the steps.

Marcus waved as the pastor backed out. "What are you guys doing here?"

"When we couldn't get hold of you, Dad called the pastor. He told us what happened. Thought we'd come to offer our help—and moral support." Mike walked past them into the living room and placed Baxter on his blanket.

"I was going to call you and see how Jeff was feeling, but then all of this happened." Marcus gave Jeff's shoulder a squeeze.

Jeff looked up at him. "All better."

Something snapped underneath Lincoln's feet. He looked down at the glass on the floor and then toward Marcus with raised eyelids.

"It's from the bedroom window. You know all about that, right?"

Lincoln nodded. "Let's get this cleaned up right away, boys."

When Marcus was settled on the sofa next to Baxter, his brothers grabbed the broom and dustpan from the hall closet.

"This probably isn't such a safe place for you to live. My nephew, Ted, is looking for a roommate. Maybe you should consider sharing an apartment with him once the house is sold. I know you'd really hit it off."

At the end of the week, Sally's voice floated through the screen door. "Hello, we came for a visit."

Marcus knew he looked terrible. He hadn't even brushed his teeth or combed his hair in days. "Did you bring Mary?"

"Yep." She walked into the room, cradling the baby against her. She laid Mary on Marcus's stomach, crossing his arms securely around the infant. Then she turned her attention to his bandaged feet. "I heard what happened. I don't know what Mr. Wilson was thinking."

A voice came from the direction of the recliner. "No one can ever know what's in another's heart."

Sally jumped. "Pastor Brice, you startled me. I didn't see you there."

"Sorry." His answer was meant for Sally, but clearly his attention was on Marcus as he held the baby and played with the tiny fingers holding onto his. "She's beautiful, Sally. Now that you're both out of the hospital, I guess the real work begins, huh?"

"I'm sure I'll find out soon enough, but the first order of business is finding a place to stay. Looks like Betty took her husband back. And he doesn't want us around. So..."

"You can stay here. It's time I cleaned out Mama's things, anyway. If you'll help me do that, we can move the crib and your stuff into her room. Mama liked pink—walls, pictures, and bedspread—just like you. You can stay as long as you need to."

"I was hoping you'd say that, Marcus. You're a true friend."

The pastor knelt beside the sofa, patting Mary's back as he studied the baby's features. "It's your business, but you two need to think this through before making such a big decision. I mean, it's admirable to want to help, Marcus, but you never know how Mr. Wilson—or Simon—is going to react. And it might not be a good idea for you two to be staying in the same house."

"How about I sleep at Frannie's—like I do most nights anyway—and I'll help out over here during the day when I can."

"That's a good idea, Marcus. Between your jobs and nights with the Johnsons, that should keep the situation—and neighborhood gossip—under control. It should also help you stay out of Mr. Wilson's way."

"I think Betty is willing to help. She'll make Mr. Wilson understand that this is the best decision.

She's already in love with Mary. She doesn't want her granddaughter sleeping on the street," Sally interjected.

The pastor rose and walked toward the door. "Well, I have prayer meeting to get ready for, so if you don't need anything else from me, I'd better get going."

Marcus shook his head. "No. Thanks, Pastor. My brothers will be here with dinner soon, and they're coming back in the middle of the week to help me with the yards I've got scheduled. Sally and I will make it just fine." He couldn't help but notice the pastor's hesitation. *And what would Lincoln say when he told him he wouldn't be moving to Tucson?*

Marcus hobbled outside to sit on the porch steps. Focusing on Mama's rosebush, he wondered what she'd think of his life if she were to see him now. So much had changed. He had a pastor for a best friend, a young girl and a baby taking refuge in her bedroom, and brothers who seemed to love him. Not to mention Betty, Frannie, and Floyd. They had helped him more times than he could count.

Then there was Mr. Wilson, and Simon. Both were predictable enemies. Each was against him, trying every way they could to make his life miserable. Why couldn't they just let him go his own way and they go theirs? And was God really expecting him to forgive them, like Pastor Brice said in Sunday's sermon? Had it been his imagination, or had the pastor been looking directly at him as he shut his eyes for the closing prayer?

Marcus observed the tall grass. He hadn't mowed this week. The yard was the worst he could ever remember it looking. Weeds had sprouted up in the planters. The roses needed water. He pushed himself up from the steps, uncurled the hose, and turned on the spigot. The water bubbled up on the parched earth, then slowly sank in.

"Can I join you?"

Sally's voice broke through his troubled thoughts just as they were turning, at last, to Lincoln. He was grateful for the interruption, since he couldn't seem to decide whether his father was friend or foe. His presence in his life was perplexing—a relationship he had yet to figure out.

"Sure. I was just giving Mama's roses a little drink." He turned off the water and replaced the hose, joining Sally on the top step.

She looked beautiful—her golden hair caught in a sloppy ponytail on top of her head, wearing a baggy T-shirt with a faded picture of Tweety Bird on the front. She bent down, attempting to massage her swollen feet.

"Here, let me do that for you." He slid down one step and put her foot between his hands. He used his thumbs to massage the arch, his eyes drawn to the chipped pink polish on her toenails.

She rested her head against the screen door and closed her eyes as he worked his strong fingers across the top of her foot and around her ankle to the heel. With each movement, her mouth curved into a slight smile and she purred just like Mango, the Johnsons' tabby.

Chapter Fifteen

The next few weeks went by quickly. Marcus divided his time between his growing lawn care business and helping with the baby. Frannie and Floyd, along with Grandma Betty, took turns, too. They did everything from cooking meals, to doing laundry, to babysitting, so Sally could work part time at a popular bakery a few blocks from the house.

Mr. Wilson was asleep in his chaise lounge under the shade of his carport when Marcus passed their house and pulled into his own driveway. As he opened the car door, his attention turned to the tiny bundle lying on his neighbor's chest. He guessed the man's irresistible granddaughter had already twisted him around her little finger.

Mr. Wilson was back living at home under the condition that he complete anger management classes at the community center and go to counseling once a week. He hadn't caused any more problems with Marcus. In fact, he paid for and replaced the broken window. *Had he just needed the right motivation to change?*

Marcus unlocked the door and pushed it open. "Sally?" The blinds were closed. Baxter was the only one who greeted him. The dog had made a miraculous recovery. The pastor had even used his story to illustrate God's healing power in his sermon the week before. Marcus would never again take his best friend for granted. That was for sure.

Marcus took Baxter out in the yard for a few minutes before coming back inside to get a package of hot dogs out of the refrigerator and start a pan of water boiling on the stove. When it was hot enough, he placed two hot dogs in the water for himself and one for Sally. She was dieting to lose her "baby weight," although Marcus couldn't see exactly what she meant by that. She looked even thinner than she had before her pregnancy.

Marcus looked at the clock. Twelve-thirty. He frowned. *Where was she?* He walked toward his room, pulling the sweaty T-shirt over his head and replacing it with a clean one from the dresser drawer. He raised the blinds, letting in the bright summer sunshine. The corner of his mouth turned up into a half-smile. Who would ever believe a simple thing like picking up a shirt folded by Sally could be a source of happiness? But it was…

His stomach growled. He walked back toward the kitchen. He'd go ahead and eat and keep Sally's hot dog in the steaming water. He pulled a bun out of the plastic bag, snagged one of the hot dogs with tongs and lathered on catsup, mustard, and pickle relish.

The first bite was heaven. He closed his eyes as he chewed. A diet of hot dogs, peanut butter sandwiches and soup—as well as pizza when his brothers visited—was all he'd had money for since he began to help with the baby's expenses. He didn't mind, really. He didn't know how to cook anything else, anyhow.

He was just cleaning up from his meal when Sally came through the door, all aglow. "Oh, did I miss lunch? I just got talking with Laura and forgot all about the time." She did a double-take as the clock's door opened and the cuckoo bird counted to three.

"Yikes, I'm going to be late. Now that you've got your license, can you drive me? I can't lose this job."

"Sure." Marcus put a squirt of catsup on a hotdog and shoved it into her hand. "What about Mary?"

Sally followed him out the door, trying to talk and chew at the same time. "Our baby and her grandpa are sound asleep, so I told Betty just to have him bring her over to you in about an hour. You'll be back home in plenty of time."

Marcus gave Sally a sideways glance as he pulled out of the driveway and headed north. Did she say *'our baby'?* Was she beginning to think of them as a little family, just as he'd often hoped she would? They both loved Mary. Was there any chance that Sally would someday love *him*, too?

"Marcus, have you heard a word I've said?"

"Why?"

"Because you look like you're daydreaming about something—and from the look on your face, it must be something pretty good."

There it was again—that hot telltale blush he couldn't control. "Oh, just thinking about seeing Mary when I get back home." He held his palm toward the air conditioning vent. "The AC must not be working. It's really hot in here."

"It's not the heat, Marcus, and we both know it." Sally batted her eyelashes at him, playfully.

"Yes, it is. What else would it be? You don't know everything, Sally Schwartz." Marcus turned his attention back to the road just in time to safely make the turn into the bakery's parking lot.

"We'll finish this discussion when I get home at ten. Frannie remembers tonight is my late shift, right?"

"She remembers. But I have a yard job first thing in the morning, so I don't think I'll have time to talk tonight. Anyway, I have to get over to Frannie's before eleven or she'll lock me out."

"Now don't you go avoiding me just when we hit on a sensitive subject, Marcus."

"What do you mean?"

"I don't have time to get into it right now. I've got a lot of doughnuts to fry and frost before my shift ends." Sally slammed the car door, ran toward the bakery, then turned, and blew him a mischievous kiss.

Marcus could hear her chuckling as she went through the door. He crossed his arms on the steering wheel and lowered his head to rest on them. He didn't know whether to laugh, cry, or wallow in his momentary happiness. Because as sure as the sun would come up in the morning, someone was bound to get hurt in all of this—and he'd bet his lawn money it would be him.

Marcus did his best to avoid Sally for the remainder of the week. It was harder to do than he'd first thought it would be because of his wanting to spend as much time with Mary as possible.

She was the most cheerful baby he'd ever seen. Other than fussing when she was hungry, she never cried. She'd kick her little legs back and forth when she couldn't contain her happiness and her cooing stopped only when she was drinking her bottle. She'd discovered her toes and spent a lot of time trying to get them into her mouth. He'd threatened to coat them with mustard, thinking it would break that habit, but Sally said if she ever caught him doing that, there would be dire consequences.

"She's all ready to go. If you'll watch her while I take a quick shower, we can be out of here on schedule." Sally placed Mary, smelling like baby lotion from her morning bath, in his arms and turned in the direction of the bathroom.

"Can't you just go to the lake without me? I don't like the water so much. Besides, I should mow for Frannie this afternoon and—" He loved their easy banter, back and forth, like true friends—like family.

"I can't hear you when I'm in the shower. You sound just like a bunch of static." Steam rose above the plastic curtain and rolled into the hallway from the partially closed bathroom door.

He loved her teasing…adored everything about her. He headed toward the kitchen with the baby in tow. "Come on, Mary. Let's put these sandwiches in the cooler and then we'll rock awhile. It'll be an hour before your mama is ready to go." Marcus placed two sandwiches into the blue ice chest they'd borrowed from Betty, cuddled Mary to his chest and gently slipped into the softness of Mama's favorite chair.

The scent of baby powder turned his thoughts to Sally and the fun they'd had at the store choosing baby shampoo, lotion and other nursery items before Mary's birth. He ran his hand across the baby's damp curls. Sally's hair would be wet, too, until it dried in today's light breeze. Her skin would smell like lilac soap…

His eyes felt heavy as he rocked gently back and forth. This was pure contentment—his dog sprawled on the sofa, whimpering as he dreamed, and Mary asleep in his arms, her little mouth working back and forth as if she were drinking a delicious milkshake—strawberry, of course.

He relaxed into a vision of Sally running barefoot in the sand, near the water's edge. Following close behind, he grabbed her wrist and pulled her to him as he studied her face. The light bounced off the water behind her as if celebrating the possibilities of what could be. If only…

"Sh—sh—don't say a word." Sally's hand clamped over his mouth, waking him abruptly. "He's back."

"Who?"

"Simon. What a surprise."

"What? I mean, how? I mean—"

"I don't know, but I just saw him through the window, getting out of a cab."

"I'm going to sneak around the back of the house and through the yard to the driveway. I'll take the sidewalk over to Betty's." She slid the sleeping baby into her arms and started out the back door. Hesitating, she turned back to Marcus, who had followed her to the door. Sally gave him a quick kiss on the cheek. "Thanks for everything, Marcus."

He caught her arm. "Wait. Does Simon know you've been staying here? Does he know we're... friends?"

"Of course not. If I'd told him, he would have been...well, let's just say he wouldn't have understood."

"But, Sally—"

"Let's talk about this another time, okay? I can't wait to see him."

Marcus watched as Sally ran between the two houses and onto the sidewalk. He crossed over to his bedroom where his window showcased their reunion—a long kiss, Simon's curious glance at Mary, Simon shaking his head *no*. Didn't he want to hold his precious baby? Marcus eased the window open. A flicker of sadness in Sally's eyes was quickly replaced by a pasted-on smile. "Of course," she said as she backed away. "I understand."

Marcus felt suddenly nauseous. *Really?* How could she possibly understand a father not wanting to cuddle his child? Marcus knew he couldn't. He clasped his arms across his chest as he slumped to his knees on the hardwood floor. *Oh, Mary.*

He was still there, a half-hour later, when he heard the back door open.

"It's me. Sally."

"Go away."

"Come on, now. I came to get Mary's clothes and formula. Please don't be angry."

He massaged the stiffness from his legs, then turned toward Sally.

She gasped when she saw his face. "Oh, Marcus. I'm so sorry." She placed her hand on his arm. "But, you knew how this was going to be, right? Simon is her father. We belong together, Marcus. You do understand this, don't you?"

"I know how it is. The guy doesn't even want to touch her. He might want *you,* but he doesn't want Mary."

"That's not true. He just needs time to get used to all this. He's going to rent us a house. We're going to be a real family. Don't you want that for us, Marcus?"

He hesitated. "Of—of course. But being happy for you? Well, I'm going to have to work up to that."

"Thanks, Marcus," she called over her shoulder as she took off down the hall. "I'm going to grab a few things and hurry back before he realizes I'm gone. I'll have to revise my schedule at the bakery and—" She disappeared into Mama's bedroom before he had a chance to respond.

Marcus crossed the hallway to the kitchen. He opened the lid of the picnic cooler, staring at the two uneaten sandwiches from the almost-picnic at the lake. He put them in the refrigerator and took out the two remaining bottles of formula. It was almost eight o'clock. He put one of them in the warmer. *Mary always drinks one right before going down for the night.*

Sally returned to the kitchen, just as Marcus was testing the temperature of the milk on his wrist. She touched his arm. "I'll try to—"

He thrust the bottles into her unzipped bag. "Just go. Have a nice life."

She reached up to touch his face.

"Don't."

Baxter cowered behind the television, a puddle of urine by the front door. Marcus rose from the sofa where he'd slept several days and nights since Sally's departure. He ejected the Spider-Man video and turned the VCR's power off. He used a paper towel to wipe up the puddle from the floor. "Come on, boy, I'll take you out. I'm not mad. It wasn't your fault." He snapped the leash onto the dog's collar and led him outside.

Rounding the corner, he almost fell when he slipped on a glossy flyer. The door of the mailbox was ajar, and several envelopes were sticking out. *Wow. How long has it been since I've brought in the mail? Or mowed the lawn?*

The phone was ringing when he returned to the house. He deposited an armload of mail onto the center of the table and took the receiver off the hook. "Hello."

"Hey, Marc. You don't sound any better than when I talked to you on Tuesday. I know you don't want to talk about whatever is wrong, but somehow you've got to snap out of it, man—"

Marcus slammed the receiver down. The last thing he needed was Mike telling him what to do. He turned on the kitchen faucet and filled a plastic tumbler. Just as he raised the glass to his lips, the phone rang again. It wasn't Mike's fault. He cared. But what could his brother do? He couldn't change the way things were any more than Marcus could.

On the fifth ring, he finally reached for the phone. "Listen, Mike, I know you mean well, but—"

"It's not Mike. It's your father. I called Pastor Brice. He'll be waiting for you in the Prayer Garden at the church in half an hour. You need to talk to someone. I don't know of anyone who's better qualified to give you advice. Listen with an open mind—and heart." The line went dead.

Marcus squeezed his eyes shut. *"I feel so alone, God. I don't care about anything anymore. Can even you save me from this awful ache inside?"* He observed his catsup-stained shirt. He shrugged his shoulders. It would do. He roused Baxter from yet another nap. "Come on boy, you can walk with me to the church."

Baxter wagged his stubby tail and circled by the door until Marcus retrieved the leash. As they approached the front sidewalk, the dog became excited, whimpering and trying to drag Marcus to the left.

"It's shorter if we cut through the neighborhood, Baxter. Let's go this way."

Baxter sat down on his haunches. He still exhibited the same stubborn streak he'd had since he was a puppy. "A dog with a mind of his own," Mama used to say.

"Oh, well, what's another five minutes going to hurt? Come on." Marcus followed Baxter as he trotted down the street. The dog seemed happy with his choice of a new route. Marcus couldn't help but chuckle as he passed the well-manicured lawns of the neighborhood to the north of his own. Perhaps Baxter was right. A change of scenery was often good for the soul. The colorful flowers and whimsical birdbaths along this route were restful. He began to feel more at peace than he had in several days.

They rounded the corner, crossed the street, and headed down the dirt bicycle path leading into yet another neighborhood. Hearing the sound of a crying baby coming through an open window, he slowed.

Could that be Mary? He crouched behind an overgrown hedge in front of a house with peeling yellow paint and a screen door hanging sideways on its hinges.

His heartbeat accelerated when the door opened, abruptly. “She cries because she doesn’t know you yet. I’ll only be gone four hours. Surely you can watch her for that long.” Sally’s familiar silhouette scurried down the steps and along the sidewalk in the direction of the bakery on Tenth Street.

Part Three

"But to you who are listening I say: Love your enemies, do good to those who hate you, bless those who curse you, pray for those who mistreat you. If someone slaps you on one cheek, turn to them the other also. If someone takes your coat, do not withhold your shirt from them. Give to everyone who asks you, and if anyone takes what belongs to you, do not demand it back. Do to others as you would have them do to you… Be merciful, just as your Father is merciful. Do not judge, and you will not be judged. Do not condemn, and you will not be condemned. Forgive, and you will be forgiven."

Luke 6: 27-31; 36-37

Chapter Sixteen

Praying for Mary's safety and happiness as he walked to the church had given Marcus some measure of peace by the time he arrived, but he still missed the baby—and Sally. What better place for him to end up today than talking with his friend in the Prayer Garden? Surely, the pastor could help him sort out his feelings.

He looked through the wrought iron gate at the overgrown and neglected garden. It needed watering and weeding. Guilt burned his cheeks. It looked almost as bad as it had the first time he'd visited there, a little over a year ago. *Before Mama died...*

He pushed the gate open, letting Baxter off the leash so he could explore. He picked up the hose, turned it on to a slow trickle and laid it in the flowerbed so the water could seep down into the cracked earth. He was pulling a handful of weeds, envisioning his fingers clutched around Simon's throat, when the pastor coughed behind him.

"Glad to see you're hard at work, but there'll be time enough to catch up on that later." Pastor Brice pulled Marcus to him in a bear hug. "Having a rough time of it, are you?"

Marcus nodded. It felt good to have someone to hold onto. "Thanks for meeting with me."

Pastor Brice took his customary seat on the bench beside the fountain. "Let's sit for a while." He reached down to pet Baxter for a moment. "Good to see you, too, boy."

Marcus ran his hand across his face. "I don't know what's wrong with me, Pastor. I just don't care about anything anymore. Simon came back home on parole and Sally and the baby went to live with him. I should be happy for them, but all I do is lay around and feel sorry for myself. I know I've got to get over it, but I just don't know how." He began to pace back and forth on the brick walkway.

"Have you talked to your family?"

Marcus cleared his throat. "My brothers are great, but I haven't really settled anything with Lincoln yet. You said we needed to talk to each other and get everything out in the open, but once Mary was born I was so happy, I just really didn't think about it." He rubbed the back of his neck, then dropped down onto the bench. "I never dreamed I could be happy again after Mama died, but Sally and the baby changed all that."

"Our lives don't stay the same, Marcus. In order for you to be able to handle changes when they come along, you'll need a firm foundation. Remember the story about the man who built his house on the shifting sand and the one who built his on the rock?"

"Sort of."

Pastor Brice pulled a worn New Testament from his shirt pocket, turned to Matthew 7 and read,

> *"Therefore, everyone who hears these words of mine and puts them into practice is like a wise man who built his house on the rock. The rain came down, the streams rose, and the winds blew and beat against that house; yet it did not fall, because it had its foundation on the rock. But everyone who hears these words of mine and does not put them into practice is like a foolish man who built his house on sand. The rain came down, the streams rose, and the winds blew and beat against that house, and it fell with a great crash."*

"Faith in God and His Word. That's what gives us hope. Is that the point?"

The pastor placed a gentle hand on Marcus's shoulder. "That's right. If we lean on Him to see us through times like these, the more we'll experience all he has for us. What *we want* will not always coincide with what is *best* for us. But if we trust Him, we will know a far deeper joy and peace than we could have ever imagined."

"I love Sally, Pastor Brice, and I love Mary like she's my own." Marcus wiped his sweaty palms across his jeans and then folded them in his lap to keep them from shaking. Had he just proclaimed his love for Simon's girlfriend?

The pastor nodded slowly. "I know you do. Right now, though, you need to step back and let God work things out. He has a plan for each one of you and it won't be so hard to accept it when you realize He knows what's best. He sees things from the beginning to the end. We can't. But we can have faith in Him and we can trust."

Marcus nodded.

"Part of building that firm foundation is getting rid of all that junk in our lives that keeps us from finding God's best. There are several people in your life that you need to clear the air with—that you need to forgive—just as God, through Christ Jesus, forgave you."

"I know you're right, but I just can't seem to do it."

"I'll pray that you'll be able to, for your sake, Marcus. Forgiveness is just as much about the *forgiver,* as it is about the *forgiven*—maybe even more so."

Several days later, Marcus leaned against the doorframe of his father's house, trying to look casual as he waited for someone to answer his loud knock. When the door opened, a startled Mike blinked in disbelief.

"Why haven't I ever met your mother, Mike?" Marcus blurted out.

"Well, hello to you, too." Mike opened the door wide, stepping back to admit Marcus into their ranch-style home. "We weren't expecting you. What's all this about?"

Marcus followed Mike into the kitchen where Jeff was eating a sub sandwich.

"Hey, Marco." Jeff jumped up from the table, giving him a big hug. Then, just as quickly, he went back to his lunch.

Mike pulled another chair over to the western-style table, motioning for Marcus to sit. "Have a sandwich, Marc? There's plenty."

"Sure. Okay." He hadn't eaten since he'd left home, almost four hours ago. He'd gotten lost driving down to Tucson, ended up in Sentinel, and had to spend the last of his money on another tank of gas. Marcus ran his hand over the brown and yellow tablecloth, noticing a collection of coffee cups on a wall shelf just above the table. He gulped, remembering the angry episode in which he destroyed his own mother's beautiful china.

Mike placed a thick slice of a sub sandwich on a plate in front of Marcus and then filled a glass with ice. "I hope Dr. Pepper all right. I'm drinking the last Seven-Up."

"Sure." Marcus poured his soda. "I like everything."

"We're glad to see you and all, Marc, but why are you here? You said something about Mom?" Mike leaned forward, sliding his chair nearer to Marcus.

Marcus ate a few bites before coming up for air. "Ah, well, that's not why I'm here, really. I came to talk to Lincoln, but while I drove I got to wondering about why I've never met her. I'm just curious. You know, about the lady our father left my mom for and all." He grabbed the bottle of soda and refilled his glass.

"This is probably something you need to talk to Dad about, but he's gone on an overnight business trip. I think you've got some of the facts wrong, though. Dad didn't leave *your* mom for *our* mom. He met our mom later. And as for why you haven't met her…it's because she left him after he got that letter appointing him to be your guardian. You were a secret until then. She had no idea you even existed."

"I don't understand."

"I know. I guess it's just that married people aren't supposed to keep secrets from each other. She said when she learned about you, it was like Dad became a whole different person than she thought she knew—a guy who'd leave his wife and newborn son—well, she just couldn't take it."

"They go counsel," Jeff interjected, looking goofy with lettuce stuck between his front teeth.

"They *might* go to counseling. *Might*, knucklehead." Mike pulled Jeff's ball cap down to cover his eyes.

"Hey," Jeff exclaimed as he reached for Mike's hat to do the same. He missed grabbing it and went toward the sink, sulking.

"We don't blame you. It's Dad's fault. In a way, he got what he deserved." Mike squished the Seven-Up can in his fist before tossing it into the open trashcan.

Marcus pushed back from the table. Lincoln should have told her about him. Still, for some reason he felt a pang of sorrow for his father. Was God opening his heart—leading him on the road to forgiveness?

"How's the baby? So cute." Jeff asked as he placed the silverware in the dishwasher.

"That cute little baby isn't *mine*. Didn't I tell you? Anyway, they're gone, Jeff. Simon is out on parole. So, Sally and Simon and Mary are just one big happy family."

Mike shook his head and then laid a gentle hand on Marcus's shoulder. "After all you did? Sally left you?"

Marcus's shoulders drooped. "It shouldn't have surprised me."

On his way to the table, Jeff gave Marcus a sloppy kiss on the cheek. "You hurt."

Marcus looked up at him with a half-smile. Tears stung his eyes. "Yeah." A bond was growing between the three of them. God had blessed him with brothers that felt his pain.

After spending the night with Mike and Jeff, Marcus headed back to Tempe. He intended to stop off at the market before picking up Baxter from Frannie and Floyd, but he was lured by the tempting aromas coming from the bakery next to it.

He walked over to the big picture window where passersby could observe the bakers mix, fold, twist, braid, bake, and frost all of their delicious creations. An older lady wearing a baker's hat removed a pan of cinnamon rolls from the oven just as Sally entered the room.

Marcus froze, unable to take his eyes off Sally's delicate features—ones that he knew almost as well as his own. She pulled a white apron over her head and tied it in one, single, well-practiced movement. When she looked toward the window, Marcus wiggled his fingers, catching her attention.

A flicker of a smile crossed her face, but instantly faded as she raised a hand to cover the right side of her face. She lowered her head and quickly left the room.

Was that a bruise Marcus had glimpsed before Sally's hasty exit? He walked around to the front of the building and pushed the heavy glass door open, the little bell at the top signaling his entrance. He rounded the counter, pushed through the swinging doors, and marched into the back room where Sally sat, crying, on an overturned barrel of powdered milk. He lowered himself to the floor in front of her and looked up at her splotchy face. He placed a tentative hand on her forearm. "Sally, what's wrong?"

Sally shook her head, reached into her apron pocket for a tissue, and blotted at the stream of mascara running down her cheeks. "You shouldn't be back here, Marcus."

"I know. Just tell me what's the matter and I'll leave. I promise."

"You'll leave right *now*, if you know what's good for you." The booming voice came from behind, followed by strong hands picking him up by the shirt collar.

Marcus stumbled to his feet. "Sally's hurt, I think."

"No, she's fine. However, she's a half hour late for the third time this week. Her appearance is unacceptable. Her hair isn't netted, and her apron isn't clean. Get her out of here. She's fired."

"No, no, Mr. Santos. I can't afford to lose this job. I won't be able to buy food for my baby," Sally pleaded.

The pudgy man in the starched apron and tall Baker's hat pointed his finger to the door. "It's the same story every day, my dear. We need workers we can depend on. You can come by on Friday to get your final paycheck."

"But, I—"

"Both of you go." His dark eyes flashed with anger. "Now. Before I call the cops."

Sally's shoulders slumped as she walked past Marcus and out the door. She plopped down on the bench across the walkway from the bakery and buried her face in her hands.

Marcus followed close behind, standing in front of her, his arms folded across his chest. "Sally, I—I'm sorry. I didn't mean to get you fired."

"I don't want to talk to you ever again, Marcus." She looked up amid sobs. "I don't want to *see* you, either."

"You don't mean that."

"I most certainly do. Simon's job at the gas station barely pays the rent. You say you love Mary, but then you go and get me fired from the very job that puts food in her mouth."

The thought that he'd brought this trouble into their lives left him speechless. He dropped onto the soft grass in front of the bench, hunched over and beat the grass with his fist. "I was trying to help. Now I've messed up everything."

"I don't know why I ever became a friend of yours in the first place. You're just a total mess up." Sally rose from the bench and walked down the sidewalk toward the corner.

When she disappeared from sight, Marcus slowly made his way toward the bakery once more—this time, with his hat in his hands.

Marcus taped the envelope to the splintered wood of the door and then set the brown paper bag on the doorstep. With one swift movement, he rang the doorbell and then jumped behind the hedge outside Sally's house. His heart pounded in his chest as he waited for her to answer the door and read his letter of apology.

When the door finally opened, it was Simon—not Sally—who peered into the sack of groceries and plucked the envelope from the door.

Oh, no. Sally's supposed to read it. Marcus's stomach churned.

Simon looked left and right before he sat down on the porch step. He stuck his finger in the flap and tore the envelope open, pulling out the lined notebook paper. His face turned crimson as he read the apology Marcus had penned just this morning.

Marcus had memorized each sentence. He'd wanted to watch Sally's face—to see her reaction to his heartfelt words. He'd planned it all out, except for one thing—the possibility that Simon would be the one to discover it. His inclination to run was thwarted by paralyzing fear.

Dear Sally,

I'm so sorry I cost you your job at the bakery, yesterday. I begged Mr. Santos to take you back, but he wouldn't listen. Here's a can of formula for the baby and a couple of bananas for you—nice and green—just the way you like them.

Marcus

"Sally, what's the meaning of this?" Simon yelled into the house, leaving the groceries on the porch step and the door open behind him.

Marcus clamped his hands over his ears to block out the sounds of shouting and glass breaking. He rocked back and forth on the withered grass until he could take no more. *Oh, dear Jesus, what have I done now?*

He stumbled to his feet and then ran down the block and around the corner. His legs propelled him in the direction of his house. Once inside, he hurried to his bedroom closet. He raked his hands back and forth across the top shelf until he felt the bulky package. He clasped it to his chest as he leaned against the door, gasping for breath.

Chapter Seventeen

The next few minutes were a blur of red and blue as the masked crusader covered the distance between his house and Sally's with superhuman speed. *Spider-Man is coming to save you, Mary Jane.*

Rounding the corner, he skidded to a stop. Smoke stung his eyes as he stared at the house, engulfed in fire. Flames licked at the downstairs windows, traveled up the front door, and marched along the roofline. *What happened here?*

A small group of gawkers stood across the street from the burning house. Four young men had formed a bucket brigade. They were already dousing flames at the front door. Another fellow, with a toddler in his arms, pointed toward an upstairs window. "I heard a baby crying and a woman screaming. We've already called the fire department."

Marcus crossed over the sidewalk and raced into the yard, taking the steps up to the house two at a time. The entire structure appeared to be ablaze. *Please God, show me the way.* He motioned the line of men aside and entered the smoke-filled house. He coughed as the air seared his nostrils and throat. Shielding his face with his forearm, he crept forward. "Mary Jane, I'm here."

His gloved fingertips followed along the wall to his right. He tried to keep his eyes closed as much as possible and let his other senses guide him into the inferno. A few steps later, he tripped over something. Groping around in the swirling smoke, he recognized the familiar softness of a body. "Mary Jane." *Thank God. Now, if I can just find the baby...*

His heartbeat raced, nearly exploding in his chest, as he grabbed underneath her arms and pulled her out of the house. Two men rushed to help him carry her to the safety of the grassy yard across the street. *Is she breathing?* His hands shook as he brushed a limp curl off of her forehead. He smiled at the sight of the wriggling and unscathed baby swaddled to her chest.

"Thanks," Sally murmured. Moments later, her eyes fluttered open. "Spider-Man?"

Marcus raised his chin, appraising the house as it sizzled in the otherwise tranquil afternoon. "Anyone else in there?"

She nodded almost imperceptibly. "Simon's... in... the kitchen...toward the...back—"

Marcus winced in pain, noticing for the first time his gloves had literally been burned off. His hands were covered in raised, red welts. *Oh, God, I don't want to go back in there. Simon doesn't deserve her. If he started this fire…*

Words he'd read just yesterday blazed in his mind's eye: *"Love your enemies, bless them that curse you, do good to them that hate you, and pray for them that despitefully use you and persecute you."*

He traced Sally's cheek with his forefinger before he left her side. He skirted along the northern edge of the house and jumped over the wire edging that separated a small garden from the rest of the yard. He could see nothing but black smoke through the kitchen window. When he turned the knob and opened the door, a blast of intense heat knocked him to the ground.

He belly-crawled forward, splinters slipping through the nylon of his suit and into the soft flesh of his abdomen. He held his breath…stifled his screams. "Simon, are you there?" He bumped against a cabinet, causing an avalanche of sizzling boards to fall from above. One landed on his back, igniting the fabric and burning into his tender skin. He gritted his teeth, trying to block out the pain and focus on the rescue at hand.

Simon's voice pierced the darkness. "Ahhhhh. Get them off me!"

"Hold tight and I'll soon have you out of here." Marcus rolled a smoldering board off Simon's shoulders and then grabbed a twitching leg and pulled with all his might. Ignoring Simon's incessant cursing, he dragged him across the cindered alleyway and safely into the neighbor's back yard. The sound of sirens filled the air as Marcus collapsed in the grass and then rolled on his back to put out the remaining sparks from his suit. Lying beside his lifelong enemy, he sucked in the fresh air.

"You should have left me in there."

"You don't know how close I came to doing just that."

"So, what stopped you?"

"Not 'what.' Who." Marcus sputtered and coughed, all the while wondering if Simon was an innocent victim or the one responsible for this nightmare.

"Mama?" Marcus was aware of someone stroking his hair throughout the night, but in the morning, there was no one at his bedside. He scanned the room, taking in the pale yellow of the walls, the cushioned chair in the far corner next to a window with its blinds partially closed. His thoughts raced, trying to make sense of what had happened…Sally's burned arms protecting her baby…Mary's cooing in the midst of the horrific fire…Simon's rescue.

Jeff and Mike popped their heads around the door to his hospital room, followed by Lincoln, carrying a fistful of colorful balloons.

"Awake," Jeff exclaimed.

Mike cleared his throat. "It's been three days. We were worried."

Marcus looked down at his wrapped hands and legs. *Three days?* Then he felt the bandage circling his face and chin with his fingertips. "My throat's sore—and everything's blurry."

"My guess is the smoke did some damage to your throat. It looks like they've put some ointment in your eyes for perhaps the same reason." Lincoln tied the balloons securely to the footboard of his bed. "What in the world were you doing in that house, Marcus? It makes no sense."

Marcus pushed the button, raising the head of the bed. Now in an upright position, he stared at his father. "It's my destiny—my purpose—to help others—"

"Really? Because I see no reason for you to put yourself in harm's way—especially for a thug and bully who has been nothing but a thorn in your side since you and your mother moved into that neighborhood—a kid who's only goal has been to make your life miserable. He belittles you at every turn, blames you for things you didn't do, and yet you go and risk your life for him."

Marcus closed his eyes, then sighed. All his life, he'd felt a kinship to Spidey—knowing that one day he'd be called to the test. He'd known he must step up... do what was required of him. But there was more to it than that now that he knew Jesus. "It's a commandment, you know—turning the other cheek—showing *compassion* to our enemies."

"Use your head, Marcus. Some people just don't deserve compassion. Plain and simple. Be smart. Turn in a new direction. Get a new life—a life without *him* in it."

"It's hard, believe me. Deep inside, I want to get back at him for all he's done, but—"

The door opened slowly, and Sally stuck her head inside. "Oops. Sorry to bother you. I can come back later."

"No, no. Come in. My father and brothers are here." Marcus's fingers felt stiff as he motioned her inside.

Sally shuffled into the room in a blue and white flowered hospital gown, Mary asleep in her bandaged arms. "Hi. Nice to see you all again."

Jeff and Mike chorused a hello, but Lincoln's face was stern and his voice sharp. "Young lady, your friendship with Marcus is most inappropriate—even unwelcome, from my perspective. He wouldn't be here, if it weren't for you."

Sally's face turned red, but she stood up to him. "I have no idea what you're talking about, but I don't have the best opinion of you, either. Marcus has told me enough to turn my stomach."

Heat crept up Lincoln's neck and reddened his face. His jaw twitched. His eyes held Sally's, as if in a vise. His nose flared, as he stood in quiet contemplation.

Mike put his hand on his father's arm. "Come on Dad, let's not get everyone all upset. Marcus needs some rest. I think it's time for us to go."

Lincoln hesitated before nudging Jeff and Mike toward the door. "Time for *all* of us to go, I think." He glared at Sally as he crossed the tiled floor, bumping her shoulder, slightly, as he exited the room.

Sally walked toward the bed. "Did you see that, Marcus? He pushed me."

"It looked like an accident." Marcus reached for Mary. "Is she okay?"

Sally placed the baby gently in his arms. "She's fine. I'm telling you, it was on purpose."

His eyebrows peaked as he considered the possibility that Lincoln cared. "Do you think he was just being protective?"

"After all those years of neglecting you?" Sally huffed.

Marcus ignored her comment. The truth still hurt. He knew full well that Simon wasn't the only one in need of compassion. After all, was Lincoln any less worthy of it than he was?

Marcus focused on Mary, awake and gurgling in his arms, kicking her legs as she stared up at him. He bit back the surging pain, but he wouldn't have it any other way. "Hi, Mary," he whispered. "How's my girl? You still know me, don't you?"

Sally sighed and shook her head. "I guess you don't want to talk about Lincoln, huh?"

"I don't. Not now—and not with you. I'll settle my differences with him in my own way…when it's time." He smiled broadly at the baby in his arms, instinctively holding out his index finger for Mary to grasp. Even though it was encased in gauze, the baby seemed not to notice.

"Let's talk about something else, then. I've been trying to put two and two together and I just can't figure out how you got hurt in the fire. What were you doing there? I don't remember seeing you. In fact, I don't remember anything much except for Simon being angry and swiping his arms across the table…things flying in all directions…and all of a sudden…fire was everywhere." Sally's eyes filled with tears.

"So, it *was* Simon who caused the fire."

"He was out of control. I don't think he noticed that I'd already lit the candles. We were supposed to be celebrating—oh, it doesn't matter—but I just can't believe he would have done it on purpose."

"You know as well as I do that when he's angry he takes it out on anyone in his path."

She nodded. "I know. I thought I understood him, but this whole incident has made me take a long, hard look at things. And I question whether it's safe for us to be around him. It will be almost impossible for me to ever trust him again," she sniffled. "I'd be pretty stupid to fall in love with a guy like him. Wouldn't I, Marcus?"

His heart double-thumped. What did she mean by telling him all of this? Now might be his one and only chance. Did he have the courage to tell Sally how he felt about her? He cleared his throat. "I've got to say this once and for all."

"You've got to say what?"

What if this costs me her friendship? What would I do without Sally and Mary in my life? Isn't friendship better than nothing? "I—um—oh, forget it."

"No, go ahead and say it. You've hated me for being with Simon—for not staying with you."

Marcus's head snapped up. Had she read his mind? "No. I could never hate you. It's nothing, really."

"Because, Marcus, you know I love you like a brother, don't you?"

He looked at her bandaged arms. "We look like twins—kind of."

"I got burned trying to keep Mary safe. What about you?"

She was trying to trick him, but he wouldn't tell her. It didn't matter, as long as they were okay. "I—uh, was just walking by and—"

"The fire spread all the way to the sidewalk?" Her eyebrows knitted into a frown, as she bit her lower lip. "Someone in a Spider-Man suit got us out of there. Did you know about that?"

"I heard."

"So, how was it that *you* got burned?"

"I—uh, don't remember any of it, either."

"Did you come near the fire? I mean, into the yard? Into the house?"

"I—I might have. But, well, does it really matter? I mean, the three of you were rescued. That's what's important, isn't it?"

Marcus pushed the door open. Betty was sitting at Simon's bedside. He backed out, slowly. He'd return later. He had things to say to Simon that were best discussed in private.

Betty turned her head in his direction. "Marcus? Come in," she whispered. "I want to talk to you…to thank you for what you've done."

"What *I've* done?" he questioned.

"You can't deny the truth, Marcus. When Sally told me what happened, I had a suspicion it was you that saved them."

He inched closer. "I just…I mean—"

"You forget I've lived next door since you were a little tyke. You were always play-acting as Spider-Man… watching those movies over and over again." Betty's eyes traveled from his head to his feet, her attention resting on his bandages. "At first, I was shocked when Sally told me *you* were hurt, but when I thought about it, I knew it would be just like you to come to the rescue." A lone tear made its way down her cheek. "But, why were you there in the first place?"

"I—well—I hadn't seen Sally or the baby in a long time. I just wanted to make sure they were all right. Guess it's a good thing I came along when I did—"

"But by saving *them*, you ended up getting hurt, too. You know, Sally thinks a Good Samaritan in a Spider-Man suit pulled them out of the fire."

"Please don't tell her the truth, Betty. I don't want them to know it was me."

"Why? You deserve recognition for what you did. You saved three lives. You should be given the Medal of Honor or something. You're a brave and caring young man. I'd be proud to have a son like *you*."

Betty's words spread warmth throughout his body. "You know how Simon feels about me. Just let it go. I don't want to start any trouble. I did what I did because I care. Can't we just leave it at that?"

"I won't say anything, but Sally has a lot of questions and she won't stop asking around until she gets to the bottom of this."

"Yeah. I suppose."

"Well, I just want to say thank you. I realize you care about Sally and the baby, but I guess I'll never know what motivated you to save Simon—after all he's done to you over the years. He's my flesh and blood and I love him—and I'm sure I don't know half of the pain he's inflicted on you—so I want you to understand how much I appreciate you rescuing our boy."

"You're welcome, Betty. You've always been nice to me. But it wasn't like I had much of a choice. God expected it of me. That's all."

"Oh, really? So, you and God are on a first name basis now. Is that it?" Simon spat out the stinging words from swollen lips.

Just how much had he heard? Marcus winced. It was just as he'd thought. Simon would find fault with anything he did—even if it was saving his life. His heartbeat quickened as he forced himself to look at the bandaged figure in the bed. He took in a deep breath. "Hey, Simon. How are you feeling?"

"I'm in pain, you moron! I'll be in the hospital for weeks. I'll be scarred for life. There's no way Sally—or any other girl, for that matter—will keep from puking when they see the likes of me. I want to die. If I ever get my hands on that Spider-Man imposter, I'll have his hide."

Betty kissed Simon's forehead and smoothed back his hair. "Son, need I remind you that guy risked *his* life to save *you?"*

"Well, it wasn't like I *asked* to be saved."

Betty placed her hand on his shoulder. "Think about Sally and the baby. Surely you didn't want *them* to die…"

Simon shook his head. "No. But in that moment, Sally made me so mad I—"

Betty's face turned ghastly pale. She took a step back from the bed, hugging her arms around her as she sank to the floor. "Simon, you—*you* did this? It was *you* that caused the fire?"

Chapter Eighteen

Since his discharge from the hospital eight days ago, Marcus had retreated back into his previous solitary life—the one he'd lived before Sally came into the picture and he'd experienced feelings he had never felt before. The days ran together like the colors of the Madres shirt he had washed without reading the care label.

He opened the paper bag the nurse had handed him when he left Tempe Community. He carefully withdrew his scorched Spider-Man costume. One arm and leg were completely gone and it still smelled of smoke. He had worn it last Halloween, but this year the holiday had come and gone without celebration. He hadn't even bought any candy to hand out.

As he held the costume to his chest, his thoughts returned to the day of the fire and the moment he'd been faced with the decision whether or not to go back into the house for Simon. What if he hadn't returned? Would he and Sally be together? Could he have avoided this broken heart?

His brothers had decided Marcus's moping around had gone on long enough—that he needed a change of scenery. So today, in spite of his protests, they were headed north from Tucson to take him out for pizza and a movie.

He reluctantly claimed a clean shirt from the laundry basket and pulled it over his head. While brushing his teeth, he thought about the last time he'd worn the blue and white Tempe High T-shirt.

He and Sally had taken Mary for a walk around the block, then ended up buying ice cream from Mr. Jerry's truck. They'd laughed and talked on the porch steps as Mary napped in her stroller.

Sally had speculated about the future and her hopes for her education once Mary was in school. The conversation had taken twists and turns down memory lane—reliving their high school years, events leading up to Simon's absence and finally their own friendship.

"You're different, lately, you know? I think Mary and I are good for you." Sally blushed as she licked her ice cream bar.

Marcus looked down at the porch steps and pushed fallen leaves off them one at a time with his forefinger. "I know you are."

Sally gave his shoulder a good-natured bump with hers. "Do you like girls, Marcus?"

"Sure. Why?" He busied himself with wiping melted ice cream off his arm, not wanting to make eye contact. He didn't want to reveal his feelings for her and he didn't want to ruin an otherwise perfect afternoon by having to deal with rejection.

"Oh, it's just that I sometimes think about how things might have turned out if Simon hadn't been in the picture..."

"What do you mean, 'the picture'?"

"I mean if you and I were, you know, 'together' –you, and me, and Mary—a little family. Living here in this house. Together."

His head spun. Could she really be saying that she cared for him—the way he cared for her? "I—I—don't know. I—"

"Oh, come on. Don't be so serious. Of course, Simon will be getting out on parole someday soon. I should be with him, no matter how I might feel from time to time—about us, I mean. He's Mary's daddy, after all."

He shook his head, spit out the remaining toothpaste and rinsed his mouth with water. Why hadn't he asked her right then if she loved him? Knowing that might have meant all the difference in the world.

But Simon *had* come back. And Sally had chosen *him.*

After the movie, what had started out as a needed diversion suddenly took a U-turn. Lincoln, who surprised Marcus by coming along, insisted on continuing their hospital conversation about Simon as they waited for their pizza at L.J.'s.

Lincoln restated his opinion that Marcus owed Simon nothing in the way of forgiveness. "I don't know much about the Bible, but I can read between its lines. You're new at this 'Christian thing.' Don't take everything so literally."

"But Colossians 3:13 says I have to forgive *him*, because Jesus forgave *me*." And not only that, but Jesus also said he must treat him as a friend...one whose life had been worth saving.

"Son, I understand the principle. But there are times when there's just too much to forgive."

Marcus had felt that way not so long ago, too. But, now he knew there was someone else he had to forgive—and that someone was sitting right here at the same table. Lincoln might never say the words that Marcus wanted to hear, but that wouldn't excuse the fact that Marcus must obey God. His voice was barely louder than a whisper. "I forgive *you,* too."

Lincoln's mouth dropped open. "I—I—don't know what to say." He cleared his throat, wiped his mouth, and brought his eyes up to meet Marcus's. "Obviously, you're the bigger man. I left—no deserted—you and your mother. It was truly unforgiveable."

"That's what I thought until just a few days ago."

"And that changed, somehow?"

"Pastor Brice showed me that there is *nothing*—and no one—who shouldn't be forgiven—no matter what they've done."

Lincoln pushed his hat back, the band soaked with perspiration. "I hope you know if I could do it all over again, I would act differently."

"You made Mama cry."

Lincoln pinched the bridge of his nose. "I know I did. She was a good woman down deep. She needed help and support instead of me leaving her on her own like that."

"She prayed every night for you to come home."

Lincoln's lips trembled. "She needed forgiveness from me. I'm sorry I never said those words to her."

"On the 'bad scale,' what you did might have been a 'ten,' but if forgiving you will give us all a chance to be a real family, then that's what I want." Marcus held out his hand toward Lincoln and both men clasped firmly.

"I'm truly sorry, son. I hope we can be best friends—like I hope I am with your brothers, here." Lincoln put his arms around Mike and Jeff's shoulders.

"*Four* Musketeers," Jeff exclaimed.

Marcus held his breath, waiting for Simon to say something—anything. This was the second hardest thing he'd ever done—on the heels of the first hardest thing—talking with his father the evening before. But he'd felt empowered by that conversation. So much so, that he'd decided not to put off the inevitable.

Simon pressed the button, raising the head of his hospital bed. "You're forgiving me? Just like that?" Simon scowled.

"It's not 'just like that.' It's one of the most difficult things I've ever had to do."

"Then why do you want to do it?"

Marcus blew out a long breath. "I don't really."

Simon cocked his head, his eyes narrowing to ominous black slits. "Then I don't understand. Why don't you educate me?" he smirked.

Marcus cleared his throat. "Jesus expects us to forgive each other. I'm just trying to obey Him."

Simon rolled his eyes. "Ah. Now I get it. You think He forgave *you*, and now you're forgiving *me?*"

Marcus nodded. "Yes, but that doesn't mean you can keep on bullying me. And it doesn't mean we have to be best friends, either."

"Then what *does* it mean, 'Mr. Holier-than-thou'?"

This wasn't easy. Simon was trying to push all of his buttons. Anger toward him threatened to surface. "It means, Mr. Big Shot, that I'm not going to hold it against you—the way you've treated me all these years. I may not be able to forget the things you did, but I won't hold a grudge or try to get back at you. I will even pray God's best for you, just like I'd do for any friend."

"*If* you had any friends," Simon spat out.

Marcus closed his eyes. *Lord, help me. I'm trying, but...* He took in another deep breath and let it out, slowly. "Think back on the lessons you learned in junior high, when you still went to church with your Mom."

"Yeah. So, what?"

Marcus reached into his hip pocket to retrieve a small New Testament that Pastor Brice had given him. As he opened it to the place he had marked, the brightly-colored book mark caught his eye. He slipped it out and read aloud: "Forgiveness is like getting a gift you don't deserve. It's called *grace*."

Simon's eyebrows knit together. "Grace?"

"Were you listening or doing crossword puzzles?" He was instantly sorry for his flippant response. "Sorry." *I've got to stay calm. If I make him mad, I won't get anywhere.*

"Neither. I was probably catching up on sleep."

Marcus laughed. He remembered seeing Simon dozing off more than once in church. "Well, I'm no preacher, but the whole thing comes down to the fact that Jesus is in my life now. So, I'm supposed to live by his example. I will go to heaven when I die. The same thing can happen for you."

Simon paused. His voice took on an almost humble quality. "That's where you're wrong, Marcus. I messed up with you and a lot of other people. I deserve punishment. Prison taught me that."

Marcus held the book out toward Simon. "This says we're *all* sinners. You may have done worse things than some of the rest of us, but to God sin is sin." He hit the cover with his forefinger for emphasis. He wanted Simon to know the words weren't coming from him.

Simon shook his head as he crossed his arms across his chest. "I don't need God and I'm sure God doesn't want anything to do with the likes of me."

"That's a cop-out and you know it. As tough as you sound sometimes, I'm betting it's just like what Pastor Brice said to me not so long ago. There's a hole in your heart that God wants to fill." Marcus cautiously laid his hand on Simon's bandaged arm. "The Bible taught me that."

Later that afternoon, as he watered the plants, Marcus thought about his conversation with Simon. Maybe he should have called Pastor Brice for support. After all, he was just a new Christian. He didn't have all the answers. The pastor would have known just what to say.

Swatting at a pesky bee as he wound up the hose and put it away in the garage, Marcus stopped abruptly at the sound of cursing coming from the Wilsons' yard. He snapped the padlock into place and remained behind the hedge, just out of view.

With the hood of his car raised, Mr. Wilson was bent over, inspecting something. Red-faced, he screamed in the direction of his house at the top of his lungs. "Now, see what you've done, Betty." He lit a cigarette, climbed inside and started the motor. "Cars need water now and then, you dimwit." He grabbed the garden hose and ran water into the radiator.

Meanwhile, Betty stumbled outside holding a towel up to her bloody face. She limped toward the car and said something to Mr. Wilson that Marcus couldn't quite make out.

Whatever it was, Mr. Wilson let the hood drop and then pushed her away with his muscular arms. He crushed his cigarette on the cement driveway and hopped back into the vehicle. The car veered down the street, steam still rising from underneath the hood.

His heart raced as Marcus rushed to Betty's side. Once he had helped her to her feet and walked her into the house, he eased her onto the cracked Naugahyde sofa and propped up her legs on the matching footstool. He rinsed out the hand towel at the kitchen sink, put ice cubes into it, and handed it back to her. "You're gonna have a shiner. Are you hurt anywhere else?"

She shook her head. "He's not one to listen to reason, as you well know."

Marcus took a seat beside her. "What was that all about?"

"He just found out about Simon starting the fire. I'm upset and angry, too, but the difference between Ed and me is that he thinks our son did it on purpose. He's threatening to disown him—and worse. I'm just glad Simon's still in the hospital, where he's safe."

Over the years, Marcus had learned that Mr. Wilson was capable of many bad things. If Simon's father wanted to hurt somebody, he'd find a way. The problem was that nobody ever stood up to him. Because they backed down, his bullying just got worse. He had hurt his family and everyone around him.

Suddenly, Marcus had an awful feeling in his gut. "I need to get somewhere, but I'll wait until Sally gets home to sit with you."

Betty glanced at the wall clock. "You go ahead. She should be home any minute. She's always here in time for Mary's bottle before her nap."

Marcus squeezed her hand. "Are you sure?"

"Oh, she'll be here. I can't believe Mary slept through all of this. It's certainly not the best environment for a little baby, is it?"

He let that question hang in the air, guessing she already knew the answer, anyway. He bounded out of the house and toward his garage.

His hands trembled as he tried to fit the key into the padlock. On the third attempt, it fell open. He heaved the heavy wooden door up with one fluid motion.

Once in the car, he thanked God that just yesterday he'd gassed up and put air in the tires. It wasn't that far to the hospital, but car trouble was one thing he didn't need. He prayed for green lights all the way.

Marcus drummed his fingertips on the steering wheel, waiting for the flagman to stop the cross traffic and give him and the growing line of cars behind him the go ahead. The clock on the dash said he'd been sitting there a full ten minutes. If he hadn't tried to take the short cut, he'd probably have arrived at the hospital by now. He wished he'd known they were replacing the sewer line on Mill Avenue.

Another five minutes ticked by before the flagman nodded in his direction. He knew better than to speed in a work zone. Mike had received the unfortunate gift of his first ticket last month, for going too fast in one in Tucson. It had a hefty fifty-dollar fine attached to it. That meant he couldn't afford to go to the rock concert. The girl he was going to take ended up accepting a date with someone else. "These things happen," Mike had said. But Marcus knew he was more than a little disappointed.

He crept along at twenty miles per hour until he was out of the zone, but then punched his foot down on the accelerator as he covered the last block to the community hospital. He parked in the first space available. He ran with the palm of his hand stretched out, signaling traffic to stop for him as he jay-walked across the street to the entrance.

He bit his fingernails as he waited impatiently for the elevator to arrive. Once inside, he had to pause again, while an orderly pushed a patient in a wheelchair into the tight space.

When the doors finally opened on the third floor, Marcus slid down the tiled corridor, rounded the corner and stopped to catch his breath in front of room 316. He shook his head when he read the sign posted in red letters on the door. "STOP: Visitor Restrictions Enforced. Only Immediate Family Members Permitted." *Why would a sign like that be on Simon's door?*

A guy dressed in green scrubs and long brown hair pulled into a ponytail, sat opposite the door. When he saw Marcus, he stood up, blocking the entrance to the room. "Don't get any ideas about sneaking in there. The sign means just what it says."

"He's a fr—fr—friend of mine. I saw him just this morning."

"That was *then*. This is *now*. Only family members allowed until his doctor says different." He crossed his arms over his chest and spread his legs apart.

Marcus took a step back. "I'm practically family."

"Well, 'practically' isn't good enough, kid."

"When can I see him?"

"I have no idea. I'm to stay here until a police officer comes to relieve me."

"A policeman?" He studied the guy's sober face for a moment before turning in the direction of the elevator. He pushed the button with the down arrow and it lit up bright red. *At least Mr. Wilson is nowhere in sight...*

When the elevator arrived, a burly policeman exited. He walked briskly past Marcus, disappearing around the corner.

Marcus made an about-face and followed him, waiting out of sight behind a snack machine. He was only able to catch an occasional word or two of his conversation with the guy in scrubs before the guy left his post, walking in the opposite direction.

Sally startled him as she emerged from the room, clutching a fist full of soggy tissues. *What is she doing here?*

The officer turned toward her with a scowl. "I'm closing this room off, young lady—official police business. Not even family is allowed from now on. I advise you to go on home or sit in the waiting room for further word." The officer dropped into a chair next to the door.

Marcus came out from his hiding place and tapped her on the shoulder. "Is Simon okay? Why can't any-one go in?"

"Geez, Marcus. Don't sneak up on me like that." Sally punched him in the arm, taking a deep breath before answering. "His dad got in here somehow. He beat up Simon pretty bad. He's in surgery."

"Then why are they guarding Simon's door? If he's in surgery, there's no one to guard."

"At first, they were going to let family wait in there. But only a few minutes after I got here, they put up that "NO VISITORS" at all sign and told me to leave." Sally's eyes took on a faraway look just like

Mama's used to when she was deciding which dress to wear to church.

"Sally, what are you thinking?"

"I'm thinking things must have changed."

Marcus swallowed hard. "What do you mean?"

"They're preserving evidence at the scene."

"Scene of what?"

Sally's lips trembled. "A possible murder."

Chapter Nineteen

The rubber soles of his shoes squeaked on the black and white waiting room tile as Marcus paced back and forth. Pastor Brice had gone to the drinking fountain down the hall for a sip of water, leaving Marcus alone with his thoughts. *Will Simon live? Does he really deserve to?*

"Let's wait a few more minutes on Betty before heading upstairs to the chapel."

Marcus jumped, startled by the Pastor's voice. "Sorry. I guess my mind was somewhere else."

Pastor Brice clapped his hand onto Marcus's back. "We all have a lot on our minds."

Betty limped through the sliding glass doors. She had a black eye and a scab had already formed on her lower lip. "Any news?"

The Pastor shook his head. "Here, sit down. You look like you might need some medical attention, yourself. Am I right?"

She shook her head. "What I really need is some good news about my son."

The pastor nodded in agreement. "You've both had a pretty rough day."

"So, you know about Ed?" She opened her purse and fished around inside to retrieve a crumpled tissue.

"Actually, he called me from jail. I talked with him for a while before coming here." The pastor's crystal blue eyes narrowed like they often did during his particularly emotional sermons. "We had ourselves a good talk. I can tell you, he's a broken man. Cried like a baby to learn he'd hurt his son so badly. He admits he needs the Lord's help. That's the best place I can think of to start."

"You don't know how long I've prayed for him to turn to God."

The Pastor nodded. "You know, forgiveness in a situation like this could do wonders."

A smile tugged at her healing lip. "I learned to do that a long time ago, Pastor. How else would I be able to live with a man like him?"

Pastor Brice put his arm around her shoulders and gave her an affectionate squeeze. "It can't have been easy all these years."

"No. We've had our ups and downs. He even left—for a period of several months—not too long ago, if you remember. His absence gave me some relief, but strangely enough, I missed the good things about him—and there are good things, Pastor, there really are. By the time he came back home, the Lord had me in a better frame of mind. I was ready to give him another chance."

The pastor took her hands in his, looking into her tired eyes. "You know, the real test may be yet to come."

Betty nodded, sobs muffled behind her hankie.

After a time of prayer in the chapel, Marcus, Betty, and the Pastor ate a late dinner in the hospital cafeteria. Betty was clearing the table of their half-eaten sandwiches when Sally joined them.

"I got Frannie to sit with Mary. I just couldn't stand to be stuck there all by myself, wondering what was going on, here." She plopped into the empty chair beside Marcus.

Marcus shook his head, wistfully. "It would have made more sense if I'd stayed home with the baby. I should've thought of that earlier."

"That's okay. I'm not complaining. Especially since I saw her roll over for the very first time just a few minutes ago." Sally's huge grin prompted the otherwise somber group to rejoice.

"I knew she'd master that pretty soon. She's been close to doing it for several days now." Betty gave Sally a hug and a tentative peck on the cheek.

Marcus listened to Pastor Brice relate the details of his own son's achievements of rolling over, sitting alone, pulling himself up to the sofa, and finally walking at thirteen months. "I didn't know you had a son. I didn't even know you were married. How come I've never met your wife?"

Pastor Brice sighed and then placed his hand over his pocket. He patted the New Testament he kept there. "My wife and son died from malaria when we were serving as missionaries in Africa. But that's a story for another time. Just knowing they are safe in heaven with Jesus is comfort enough for me. When the time is right, I'll share that story with you. It's a perfect example of how God is able to take bad circumstances and turn them into good. Don't ever believe He can't turn things around and use them for His ultimate purpose—'cause He can."

Marcus nodded. He understood that God was all-powerful. He hoped God would choose to use some of that power to heal Simon. Strange that he felt so deeply about a guy who'd been tormenting him since childhood and who was now standing in the way of Marcus and true love.

He couldn't quite understand it, but he was starting to care for the guy in spite of himself. The more he prayed for him, the more he genuinely wanted Simon to live. Oh sure, he could make a case for the fact that Simon didn't deserve Sally. Nobody would say otherwise—even Simon's own mother. But Marcus knew love was complicated and that most people were helpless to turn it away when it came knocking on their door.

He would have sworn that Sally loved Simon. But after the way she'd been talking lately, what was Marcus to think? He flinched when he felt her smooth fingertips grasp his hand underneath the table.

At two o'clock in the morning, Marcus turned the key in the lock. The house was dark, except for moonlight spilling in through the open blinds. Walking toward his bedroom, he was mesmerized by the horizontal patterns they made on the hallway walls. He'd never noticed them before. But, then again, everything looked different tonight…

Baxter was asleep at the foot of the bed, his tongue hanging out of his partially-opened mouth. Even Marcus crawling into bed didn't waken him.

He shut his eyes, but though his body was tired, he just couldn't doze off. All he could do was relive Sally's unexpected touch. When she'd grabbed his hand, he'd felt heat travel to his face and his mouth go dry. From that moment on, he hadn't heard another word that was said at the table. His thoughts had shifted to the beautiful girl sitting next to him, imagining they were the only two people on earth.

It wasn't as if he hadn't ever thought about the possibilities of them being together. Then why did he feel guilty for enjoying a few brief moments of happiness? Maybe it wasn't guilt at all. Maybe he was simply guarding his heart. Because he was certain all of this would end once Simon was released from the hospital.

After tossing and turning for over an hour, he finally gave up and went to sit outside on the porch steps. The air was crisp and cool. It was perfect sleeping weather, but he couldn't rest.

He turned at the sound of the Wilsons' door opening. Light shining through the screen illuminated the fluffy slippers Sally had commandeered the first night she'd spent in his mother's bedroom. They slapped against the concrete as she walked to the end of Betty's porch. She sang quietly to the fussy baby in her arms, stopping only to kiss the top of her head, then pick up the sweet melody again.

Marcus slid back into the shadows, not wanting to interrupt this tender time shared by Sally and her little one. She was already a good mother. She deserved to have the support of a loving husband...a good provider...someone who'd grow to love Mary as his own. Would she allow *him* to be that person?

He'd heard it said that love was a decision. He guessed that was true because he'd decided to love Sally in spite of her fickle ways. He couldn't see anything ever happening that would cause him to change his mind.

The phone ringing next door interrupted Marcus's thoughts. Sally rushed to answer it, letting the screen door slam behind her. Could it be news of Simon? No, they'd already heard that surgery hadn't been necessary after all. In fact, they'd even been allowed a brief visit with him after he'd returned to his hospital room. *In a few days, he'll be coming home...*

Only minutes later, Marcus's own phone rang. He jumped up and ran inside, catching it on the third ring.

"It's Sally."

"Is something wrong?"

"Simon's gone."

Marcus gasped. "What do you mean, 'gone'?"

"He's missing from the hospital."

"D—did you tell Betty?"

"Yes. I woke her up. She's pacing the floor, trying to think of what to do."

"I'll be right over. I know exactly what to do."

The baby, asleep in her infant seat, held Marcus's attention. "Mary's so cute. I like the funny faces she makes while she's sleeping. Do you think she's dreaming?"

Sally shrugged her shoulders. "That's what some people think."

"Doctors say it's just gas." Betty brought a stack of buttered toast to the table.

Marcus felt his face grow warm as he stifled a laugh. He turned back to his plate of scrambled eggs and bacon. "I'm glad we prayed. Wherever Simon is, I'm sure he's safe."

"Me, too." Sally said between sips of orange juice.

"Why is it that praying seems to be the last thing we usually think of doing? It's like we try everything else and then resort to prayer when all else fails. Leave it to new Christians to remind us old-timers to take everything to the Lord in prayer…" Betty patted his hand and then reached for the coffee pot. "Simon will come back home when he's ready. My guess is that he has a lot of soul-searching to do."

Sally shook her head as she gathered the plates and headed toward the sink. "Yes, but what a crazy thing to do. He still needs medical care."

Marcus stood and stretched. "I'd better get to the Grangers'. I've got both their front and back yards to do today. I'll keep my eye out for Simon while I'm driving across town. Thanks for breakfast, Betty."

Betty held the screen door open for him. "I'll stay near the phone today. He may call."

Marcus turned back toward Sally. "Do you work today?"

"No. Mary has a doctor's appointment. Her shots are due again. Maybe when we're done there, I can check with a couple of Simon's friends. I was going to start looking for the guy who saved us from the fire—you know, to thank him—but I don't know why I can't look for them both at the same time."

Marcus swallowed the lump in his throat. "I thought you said Spider-Man saved you."

"What I meant was a *guy in a Spider-Man suit* saved us."

"Wh—wh—what are you saying?"

"The 'real' Spider-Man isn't *real.* He's just a comic book character."

A sinking feeling pierced Marcus's stomach. "I—uh are you sure about that? He's done so many brave things and there's—"

Sally frowned. "You knew he wasn't real, didn't you Marcus?"

Could he have been that stupid? What about Superman? Wasn't he real, either? He walked home in a daze and headed for the living room. Baxter hopped off the sofa to greet him. He buried his face in the dog's soft fur, ignoring Sally's incessant knocking on the door behind him.

Marcus waved goodbye to Mr. Jensen. Another in a long string of people that had come to see the house. None of them had been interested in buying it—and that was just fine with him. He liked it here. He had more than one reason to want to continue living next door to Betty.

He could smell rain in the air. The wind had already begun to blow and the sun had gone behind the black clouds. Marcus snuggled Mary to his chest when a loud clap of thunder startled her. He returned to the house and headed for the closet.

Once inside, he placed Mary on his lap facing him. He could soon hear the rain on the roof and the slapping of wet leaves against the bedroom window. He recoiled at each crash of thunder, causing the little one to cry. He shushed her, jiggled her, and offered her the pacifier. But nothing seemed to work.

He was glad he'd already finished the Grangers' yards by the time the sky darkened. It was his afternoon to keep Mary, so he'd had good reason to hurry with his work and get home early. Now he had to find some way to soothe her until the monsoon storm blew over. He and his mother had always weathered them in this very closet. It had comforted him, so why wasn't it working on Mary?

"I know, let's play your favorite game." He brought her hands together, then apart, then together again. "Pat-a-cake, pat-a-cake, Spider-Man. Save Mary from the fire as fast as you can."

All of a sudden, the door slid open. Sally stood in front of him, her hair and clothes soaking wet. She dropped to her knees. "Marcus, didn't you hear me calling you? What in the world are you guys doing in here, anyway?"

"I, uh—we, my mom always kept us safe in here when it rained. I'm not sure if it was because she was afraid, or she thought I was. It doesn't seem to be comforting Mary, though."

Sally snagged a folded towel from the stack of clean laundry and wrapped it around her. Then she squeezed into the closet beside him and closed the door. "It's sure spooky in here. I would think the dark would have frightened you more than the sound of thunder."

"Yeah, I suppose. But it didn't. Mom and I would just sit here and talk or sing songs to pass the time. Funny. It's one of my best memories."

"Did she talk about how to be brave—like Spider-Man?" Sally reached for Mary, brought her up to her shoulder, and patted her back until she quieted.

"What do you mean?"

"I mean, I heard your little chant about Spider-Man through the closet door."

"Oh." Marcus lowered his head.

"It was *you* that saved us from the fire, wasn't it?"

"Ever since I was a little kid, I've looked up to Spidey. Now I know how stupid I was to think he was real, but—"

"No." Sally gave his hand a squeeze. You needed a hero in your life. He gave you courage. How could that ever be a bad thing? If it hadn't been for him, you might not have acted on your instincts and saved us."

"I hope Spider-Man never finds out I hide from storms in my closet."

Sally laughed. "You're still talking about him as if he's real, Marcus."

"Oops. Well, I can't help it. I guess he'll always be my hero."

"And I guess you'll always be mine."

His heart double-beat. "Really?"

"You saved three lives. That's pretty impressive. And, to be truthful, I suppose I need a hero in my life, too…someone to keep Mary and me safe…someone to love… someone who will be brave enough to kiss me right here in his closet in the middle of a rainstorm…"

"Wh—wh—what? You want me to—?"

"Yes. Right now—before I change my mind. You're my Spider-Man and I'm your Mary Jane. Kiss me, *now*."

Chapter Twenty

What kind of a letter is this? A Christmas card, maybe? Marcus pulled a small envelope with no stamp and no return address out of his mailbox. *'MARCUS'* was written in large red letters on the front.

He scratched his head. Was somebody playing a joke? He looked down the street one way and then the other. He shrugged his shoulders and then reached inside the box to gather the rest of the mail. With one last glance over his shoulder, he went back into the house.

Even though it had been almost two weeks, the kiss between Spider-Man and Mary Jane dominated his thoughts. He poured milk on his cereal, grabbed a spoon from the drawer and sat down at the kitchen table. Not even a mysterious letter could pull his attention from the memory of his first kiss. He'd seen Sally several times since then and each time he thought she looked like she might be sharing similar thoughts. Would she say "yes" to another kiss, if he'd make the first move?

A soft knock on the front door interrupted his first bite of Cheerio's. Letting his spoon drop into the bowl, he shuffled into the hallway. Someone else was up early on this very first morning of winter.

Before he reached the door, Sally turned the knob and breezed past him. She pulled off her sweater and hung in on the hall tree in the corner of the living room. "Guess what was in yesterday's mail?" She hurried toward the kitchen, rubbing her hands together and blowing on them with short breaths. "Is there any coffee left? It's getting chilly out there."

The fragrance of lilacs filled the air, stirring the memories of her lips against his. He felt his cheeks warm and familiar butterflies swarm in his stomach. He followed her like a new puppy into the kitchen where she grabbed a cup from the drain board and filled it from the coffee pot. She took a sip before dropping into the chair across from Marcus. She retrieved an envelope from her pocket and thrust it into his hand.

He frowned. It was just like the one he'd received. He studied the word *'SALLY'* scrawled across the front.

"So, what do you make of that? Crazy, huh?" Sally drummed her fingertips on the Formica.

"You're not going to believe this." Marcus retrieved his envelope from the counter and handed it to Sally.

"You got one, too?"

"Yeah. Just alike, aren't they?"

"Except that mine says 'Sally' and yours says 'Marcus'."

Marcus rolled his eyes. "Funny." He compared both letters. "The handwriting is the same."

"Yeah. Simon's."

"Really? Have you read yours?"

"Nope. I was scared to. I mean, maybe he's coming back. Come to think of it, with no stamp on it, he probably *is* back..."

Marcus's heart nearly stopped beating. He felt all life drain from his body as he slumped against the back of the chair. This couldn't be happening. Did Simon somehow know about him and Sally? Did their envelopes contain some kind of threat? He looked into her somber eyes—eyes that revealed what he already knew to be true—she was just as afraid as he was.

"Let's read them together. We'll flip a coin and whoever wins gets to choose which one we'll open first. Okay?" Sally furrowed her forehead, waiting for his response.

Marcus nodded and then retrieved a nickel from the change jar. "Heads or tails?"

"I'll take heads."

"Okay, here goes." He flipped the coin into the air. When it landed in his palm, he placed it on the back of left hand and covered it with the other. He looked up at Sally. "Ready?"

She gulped and then nodded. "Let's see it."

Marcus peeled his hand away, revealing Jefferson's head. "You win. What will it be?"

Sally tapped her fingers mischievously against her lips. She slipped her envelope back into her pocket. "Let's read yours first."

His hands shook as he spread his letter out on the tabletop between them. He followed along as Sally read aloud.

Marcus-

I guess I'm like my father after all. I run from responsibilities. And, yes, I know that Mary is *my responsibility. When I am able to work, I will get a job and send Sally something for her each month.*

I know Mary is mine, but I don't feel like a dad. I think if I stay around I might end up treating her and Sally bad. Maybe the fire was a sign that I can't handle anger all that well.

I've seen the way you and Sally look at each other and I'm guessing that you'd be together if it weren't for me. Or, maybe you've already been together behind my back. I wouldn't put it past either of you. By the way, she's used goods, if you know what I mean...

I expect you both to let Mom continue to see the baby. I know she loves being a grandma.

The shrink at the hospital said people who are abused often end up taking their anger out on someone else. I still don't understand how you could forgive me for treating you like that because I know I can't forgive my dad.

Simon

As they finished reading the letter, Marcus looked up at Sally. She was quiet—too quiet. Hadn't she felt the sudden freedom that he had? He swallowed hard. "Well, how about that?"

Sally cocked her head and drew her eyebrows together, deep in thought. Finally, she placed her hand on his. "Let's see what his letter *to me* has to say." She retrieved the envelope and tore it open.

Somehow reading a letter intended only for Sally made his stomach queasy. He raised his eyebrows. "Here goes."

Dear Sally,

You know I love you, girl—and Mary, too—but not the way I should or in the way you deserve. You were the prettiest girl in school… not the smartest, though, because you got mixed up with me.

I hope you won't think my leaving is deserting you. It's just my way of letting you go so you can have a better life than you would if you were stuck with me.

I think you might have feelings for Marcus. He's an ok guy. You could do worse.

Don't feel guilty about finding happiness. I know I won't, if I ever find it.

Give Mary a kiss for me.

Love,
Simon

"Well, I never expected that." Sally left the table; then snagged a Kleenex from the tissue box on the counter. She leaned against the cupboard, dabbing at her eyes with trembling fingers.

The silence was almost unbearable. His heart raced. What was she thinking…feeling? Were those sad tears, or happy ones? Was she disappointed? Relieved? Confused? Did she still love Simon? *Didn't our kiss mean anything?*

And then, in slow motion—just like in the movies—she walked toward him with the hint of a smile on her face.

Epilogue

The Community Room at the Tempe Public Library was packed. Only a few chairs remained empty. That, and the fact that it was a day for record-breaking heat, made Marcus feel lightheaded.

He'd never spoken to a large group before. Not even the nerves that had accompanied oral book reports at school could compare to this. His heart felt like it would beat out of his chest. His eyes searched the audience, hoping for familiar faces. He spotted Lincoln, Jeff, and Mike in the back row. He needed all the support he could get, but had cautioned Jeff to refrain from cheering, as was his habit when they went to the movies and his favorite actors appeared on the big screen.

The long hand on the clock at the front of the room pointed straight up. Seven o'clock. He gulped as the librarian rushed to the microphone and tapped it with her forefinger. He jumped along with half of the audience when it squealed.

Mrs. Whipple cleared her throat, a smile pasted on her plump face. "Culminating our month-long community awareness campaign on bullying and its effects, this evening we have the pleasure of hearing from Marcus Lickenberger." She waited until the crowd's enthusiastic applause subsided before continuing.

"Neighborhood children began bullying Marcus as a young child. He's not here to name names or cast blame. Rather, he is going to simply share how being a victim of this cruel treatment affected his school work, his relationships, his physical and emotional health. Despite being mistreated, at the age of eighteen he became a local hero by rescuing several people from a house fire just a few short blocks from here. Please hold comments and questions until he has finished speaking. Let's give Marcus a warm welcome."

With knees wobbling, Marcus walked toward the podium, shaking hands with Mrs. Whipple before she took her seat in the front row. What had ever made him think that he could speak in public about those things that had shaped his life up to this point? Could he really share the humiliation with these strangers? He clenched the microphone in a stranglehold.

Sally had encouraged him to accept the librarian's invitation, saying that relating what he had gone through would help others—that talking about his ordeal in public would aid in the healing process for him, too. She'd been so sure about all of it that he'd finally given in and answered Mrs. Whipple's kind letter.

Sally had helped him outline his speech, listened to his presentation every night for four weeks, and finally pronounced him "ready." He was counting on her for moral support tonight. He'd put a RESERVED sign on a seat for her in the middle of the room, where he could see her easily, but it had somehow been removed. Now, it was occupied by a bearded guy wearing glasses and a baseball cap. Marcus paused. There was something about those eyes. *Could it be—? No. Simon is long gone.*

His heart started to pound. Where was she? Surely, he wouldn't have to go it alone. No one could know how desperately he needed—

Movement at the back of the room caught his attention. The Pastor, followed by Sally, Mary, and Betty, squeezed past his father and brothers, taking the last three vacant seats. When they were settled, Marcus waved at Mary who was already bouncing energetically on her grandmother's lap.

Their encouragement was all he needed to calm his fears. He took a deep breath and licked his lips. "Good evening, ladies and gentlemen. My name is Marcus Lickenberger, but I was known by most of the kids in the neighborhood—and at school—as Marcus Lickenbooger. It was a name given to me by a bully when I was only seven years old.

My earliest memory of being bullied was on my first visit to the ice cream truck, although I didn't know it was called 'bullying' back then. To me, it was just someone being mean to me—someone I didn't know—someone who didn't know me. I guess that's part of the injustice of it all. Bullying is completely undeserved."

For a full hour, Marcus shared his story. At times, he stopped to regain self-control…to wipe at escaping tears…to smile sheepishly at Sally when he talked about meeting her and their budding relationship. Of course, the latter information clearly veered from the agreed-upon script, but from the blush on her face, he knew she didn't mind.

"I have forgiven those who bullied me. I did this out of obedience to God. It changed my life and gave me the courage to tell my story here tonight."

Questions following his speech lasted until almost nine o'clock. Although Lincoln and the boys were invited to join them at Betty's house afterward, they headed back to Tucson instead. Mike had an early class at the community college the next morning.

When the last of the audience had filed out the door, Marcus followed the librarian to the back exit. After she clicked off the lights, one row at a time, he shook hands with her and then headed on his way to Betty's for a slice of celebration pie. He thought his heart would burst with happiness when he rounded the corner and an arm slipped around his waist. He rested his hand on Sally's shoulder and then lowered his head to plant a kiss on Mary's curly hair. "Hi, squirt."

Mary wriggled in Sally's arms. "Want down." She reached out to Marcus.

"Yes, of course. You're such a big girl now. Mommy can take one hand and I'll hold the other one, so you can stay safe on this busy street. Okay?" Mary was almost three, and he was thankful that she'd soon be out of the demanding "terrible two's" stage. Her love of playing hide and seek had caused them several anxious moments over the past several months.

"You did a great job tonight. I'm very proud of you, Marcus." Sally gave his hand a squeeze and then fell in step with him.

"I couldn't have done it without you."

They walked on in silence, passing the baseball field and then the hospital. They instinctively slowed as they approached the park where nearly four years ago she had poured out her heart to him about her pregnancy.

"Can pie wait for a few more minutes?" Sally motioned toward a bench. "Sit with me?"

He slid his arm along the back of the smooth wood and settled on the seat next to her. Without him being aware of it, the nervousness leading up to this night had lifted and had been replaced with a quiet assurance that things were right in his world.

Mama had prayed for a special friend for him, but instead God had given him three amazing and supportive individuals. He also had solid ties with his brothers and a growing relationship with his father. He still missed Mama—he guessed he always would. But for now, he'd cling to the promise that God was working "all things together for good."

"Lincoln told me that your house is finally out of probate."

"That's right. He says I've proven myself to be responsible, so he will let me be the one to decide whether to sell it or not. My landscape business has grown so much that I can even afford to buy another house that's a little larger if I want to."

Sally nodded, her eyes twinkling. "You can always stay where you are right now until you're sure. Mary and I will be just next door. I'll be working during the day—and you and I will be taking our G.E.D. classes on Thursdays—but we'll still have enough time to start writing your book in the evenings."

"Book?"

"Sure. Telling your story tonight was just the beginning."

"I guess that's another thing to put on my prayer list."

Sally grinned. "What else is on that prayer list of yours?"

Marcus looked up at the sky. He couldn't remember ever seeing it crowded with so many twinkling stars. Was this the right time to bring up the subject that had been on his mind for the past few months?

He slipped his hand into the pocket of his brown corduroy blazer. His heart raced as his fingers fumbled to retrieve the smooth circle of gold with the small diamond that Lincoln had given Mama nearly thirty years ago.

He drew in a deep breath and then lowered himself onto one knee. He took Sally's hands in his as he brought his eyes up to meet hers. "There has been something special on my mind…"

Dear Reader

I consider it a great blessing to communicate the power of God's love through my writing. As Christ forgives us, I believe we are to follow his example by offering forgiveness to others.

I trust the story of Marcus and the scripture verses contained in *Simon Says* will encourage you as you face obstacles in your relationships with others. I pray that you will receive God's richest blessings as you practice forgiveness in your own life.

In a world filled with injustices and hatred, may we each be examples of how faith and love can heal brokenness and create meaningful lives based on the truth of God's Word.

Thank you for reading *Simon Says.*

Brenda C. Poulos

About the Author

Brenda C. Poulos is a former regular education, special education and elementary school guidance counselor in Arizona. She and her husband have four adult children, seven grandchildren, and two furry critters that enjoy napping and brief games of *seek and find*.

In addition to writing, Brenda enjoys working with her husband on home renovations, traveling, watching movies, and reading.

Brenda's Christian fiction books include: *Runaways: The Long Journey Home, The Choice: Will's Last Testament, and Simon Says.* She has also published two interactive picture books for Alzheimer's patients,

I Remember the Seasons, and *I Remember Bible Stories.* Also available are Kindle devotional books, *How Deep His Love*, Volumes One and Two.

Brenda is a member of American Christian Fiction Writers and past president of Christian Writers of the West. She is also a church, hospice and elementary school volunteer.

As a Christian author, Brenda's goal is to communicate God's love and grace to her reading audience. Her stories of forgiveness offer hope to readers worldwide.

To find out more about Brenda, her books, and her writing career, please visit www.brendapoulos.org, www.spiritualsnippets.com, Facebook, Twitter @MTNSTBrenda14, Goodreads, Amazon's Author Central, and Booklaunch.

Please review *Simon Says* on Amazon.com and Goodreads.

Other Books by Brenda C. Poulos

Runaways: The Long Journey Home

The Choice: Will's Last Testament

I Remember the Seasons

I Remember Bible Stories

How Deep His Love, Volumes 1 & 2

Made in the USA
Monee, IL
26 January 2020

20891917R00140